AF427886

The Genesis of Fallibility:
Stories from Martinsburg, Indiana

by

Séafra Duffy

TYPEWRITER FOX STUDIOS

2022

For Roberta...

...because she supported me

when no one else did.

TABLE OF CONTENTS

Reconnections..........…..…...............…...…1

Rabbit Holes…….………….……….…...23

Hoosier Crossroads…….…..........…......35

Plot E…..……………….…….…........53

Rock-A-Bye-Baby……...….…….…....67

Room 302…….……….….……….......81

A Smile in the Sunshine…..……….....93

The Genesis of Fallibility……..…......103

Martinsburg, Indiana

Martinsburg, Indiana is a stereotypical mid-sized Midwestern town, nestled behind a protective buffer of corn and soybean fields insulating it from the hustle and bustle of Indianapolis, directly to the east. Crime, while not strictly unheard of within its town limits, remains statistically low for the two hundred and fifty thousand residents who call Martinsburg their home.

Platted in 1832, Martinsburg did not fully blossom until shortly after the Civil War, finally being incorporated in 1867. The growth in transportation and manufacturing during the vibrant post-war economy helped forge Martinsburg into a darling of Central Indiana. Many prominent members of the Indianapolis social elite called it home for parts of the year to avoid the smoke and noise of the state capitol.

As with most of the Midwest, the fortunes of Martinsburg ebbed and flowed in the tide of the national economy. It enjoyed the boom years by undertaking ambitious social improvement projects, and the residents patiently persevered through the bust years with typical Hoosier determination. Overall, Martinsburg made steady economic progress and maintained an upward trend, never losing its grip upon a moderately comfortable level of success and tranquility.

It was supposed to be a comfortable place to raise a family.

But as is all too common in most larger Midwestern towns, Martinsburg holds within its demographics a microcosm of modern American society, comprising a range of people and disparate levels of prosperity. There are the well-off social elites living in their gated, electronically protected neighborhoods to the north and east of town. The less fortunate citizens live their trailer park existence in the southern sections of Martinsburg. Over to the west, a comfortable middle class sprawls, generally remaining silent unless someone attempts to raise their property taxes.

But the lines between classes seldom transcribe so precisely onto a map. There are certain areas of Martinsburg where they sometimes overlap and clash, creating striking stories amidst the streets and alleys of "just another flyover town."

What follows are some of those stories...

Reconnections

I

"OMG! That really U?"

Daniel wasn't sure which annoyed him the most, her abbreviated texting etiquette, or the rather speedy way she was replying to his social media private message, ill-advisedly sent while nostalgically drunk the night before.

In the suffering of his hangover, Daniel was unsure what had even sent him down that rabbit hole, sometime after that Dylan album had finished and the second bottle of his favorite whiskey had been opened. His divorce was long behind him. Work had pushed him into an inescapable backwater of professional mediocrity. Life had been going- okay. The stagnation of his nights a never changing tapestry of Midwestern blandness. The daylight hours playing out predictably grim, like some low-budget Turner classic movie stuck on repeat.

It left Daniel feeling hollow.

Initially, he tried filling those introspectively cancerous hours with a bottle for company. When that failed, Daniel took to trying various narcotics, legally prescribed to *someone*. He was far too old for negotiating the seedier exchanges of a back-alley Martinsburg, Indiana drug deal. Instead, Daniel took the responsible course of pestering his friends and coworkers to share their prescriptions. The time for street-level stupidity had passed

1

when Daniel exchanged his youthful freedoms for a laminated card proclaiming his new identity in a structured, soul-crushing 9-to-5 universe of pointless presentations and terrible coffee.

But the night before had been a perfect Midwestern storm of bad decisions.

Work had been awful that claustrophobic Friday and it drained Daniel's soul away in another salaried bite. A stack of bills, overdue and angry, taunted him when Daniel returned home. Utilities were going to start being disconnected and payday was another week away. Based upon the screeching message on his machine from his recent ex-wife, Daniel secretly hoped that it would be the not-often-used landline phone that would be the first utility sacrificed.

There were mental flashes of stalking the social media pages of the Martinsburg Central High group, sometime well into that second bottle. The light-weight voice of reason had passed out early, just like it always does, leaving no filters to catch Daniel from making his bad decisions. Instead, Daniel poured out his heart in a poorly paragraphed, whiskey-fueled private message diatribe.

And he actually hit the fucking SEND button.

Daniel Wagner and Kimberly McCleary were quite the couple back in the grungy days of Martinsburg Central High School, class of 1994. They had started dating in their sophomore year and, while not moving in the circles of the Central High social elite, they were still popular with their classmates.

Their relationship followed the trajectory that most high school romances take while burning through their inevitable arc of hormonal exploration. Sometimes, the coupling ran hot and seedy. Other times, it chilled considerably in their mutual navigation of the tumultuous social currents of a Midwestern high school. But most of the time, the young couple were caught between the two extremes. Some of their classmates even whispered that Daniel and Kimberly might go the distance and continue dating on into college.

Kimberly was Daniel's first real girlfriend and, after reaching a certain point in their relationship when the patterns had become entrenched and the conversations predictably stale, Daniel began to wonder what, and more importantly, who, else might be out there for him. He felt compelled to answer the siren song of better potential calling to the heated hormones of his indecisions and it pushed Daniel to eventually break things off rather abruptly with Kimberly.

Kimberly was blindsided by Daniel's "We need to talk" conversation, shared that hot day after school while walking across one of the many bridges in Washington park. They started that walk hand in hand. By the end, they parted as two separate people, destined for opposite directions, violently un-coupled in the brutal selfishness of an unforeseen hormonal shift.

She was devastated.

Kimberly loved Daniel with all her heart and knew, even though she was only 17 years old, that Daniel was "the one." The man she was destined to one day marry. The one she wanted to build a family with, nuclear and durable. The one who had given her his virginity that cool fall evening along the same back paths of Washington park.

They lost track of one another shortly after high school graduation. But their destinies ended up being shockingly similar. Both Daniel and Kimberly ended up enduring a seemingly endless series of bad, abusive, or mediocre relationships.

Through it all, Kimberly always thought about Daniel.

He was the one who got away. Through most of her other relationships, she held Daniel up as the standard against which no other man could seemingly measure. And that elevation ultimately made her unhappy, despite the smile she tried to keep plastered on her face for the sake of her daughter, Hannah.

Daniel did not often think about Kimberly. Not soberly, anyway. But apparently the right mixture of professional disappointment, personal relationship tragedies, and mid-tier whiskey is the catalyst required to reignite ignored memories.

At least he was man enough to apologize for his youthful callousness in his drunken message, Daniel thought to himself while scanning the conversation. He was confused as to why his drunken subconscious chose to finger open that particular Pandora's box. But, judging from the vibe of her reply, coupled with the blushing, winking emoji tagalongs, Kimberly's box was at the very least receptive to Daniel's sudden and unexpected social penetrations.

Daniel just wasn't certain if he wanted to be with Kimberly again.

After his divorce, he had been on a determined anti-relationship kick. And, she had gained some weight in the twenty plus years since those mutually trim days of their high school glory years. Not that Daniel had remained rail thin, either, rounding himself out nicely into the quintessential Midwestern dad physique. He just preferred his ladies a bit on the thinner side.

She also had a kid. That much could be inferred from Daniel's hungover social media stalking. And he wasn't sure how he felt about entering that minefield of a single mother's parenting responsibility.

But Daniel also knew that a night full of awkward reintroduction was better than a morning filled with empty boredom. So, he sent a brief reply.

"Hello. Yes, it really is me. How are you?"

From those innocuous nine words sprang the reconnected romance of two former high school lovers. Kimberly had the opportunity to again be with the man of her dreams. Daniel was afforded a warm body against which to sleep, protectively sparing him from the naked disappointment of sleeping alone.

It worked- for a while

They unknowingly providing the other with the emotional attachments they most needed. Or that they were willing to settle for in a last-gasp, midlife crisis sort of way.

Both instinctively knew that time was growing short. So maybe this was as good as they could reasonably expect out of life.

It helped that Daniel did end up bonding with Hannah.

It took them some time to grow comfortable around one another. But once they had established their boundaries through cleverly worded teasing insults, they connected- tightly.

Daniel tried his best to bond with Kimberly, too. But it did not take him long to remember why he had walked away from her the first time- Kimberly was boring.

Not annoyingly boring. But more of a mundane, suburban single mom dial-tone kind of boring. The animosity that Daniel felt at finding himself ensnared in the predictable pages of her story again bubbled just under the surface, waiting for the rupture's tear.

It wasn't long before they weren't really talking. The sex quickly became scheduled and mundane. Every attempt made to recapture their more youthful spark continually fizzled out, one time in showers of vomit expelled from a blackout drunk Kimberly, gurgling and rocking back and forth on the microfiber couch.

But Daniel's relationship with Hannah had improved as she slowly learned to trust him. He never raised his voice to her like her divorced parents often did in their conflicting co-parenting cacophony. Daniel mostly just listened and he seemed to have a knack for phrasing his honesty in such a way that it mitigated any unintended sting. Hannah felt like Daniel treated her as a grown-up. Perhaps not quite as an equal, but certainly as someone for whom Daniel felt genuine affection and concern.

Hannah was not initially prepared to have such a reasonable, stabilizing influence in her life. At first annoyed that her mother had found someone else with whom to share her time, Hannah began acting out against the change in the household dynamic. Invented injuries. Nonsensical stories of her high school social life pitfalls. The age-inappropriate tantrums thrown because her mother had bought the wrong kind of burrito at the store, leaving Hannah with nothing to eat in her picky defiance.

Daniel met all that hormonal teen girl drama and angst with a quiet stoicism. He simply handled his day and tried his best to help Hannah's mother handle hers, too. He was there to contribute around her house. Daniel was the one who proposed those family walks after dinner. He wanted to take 30 minutes from the hustle of building a life together and to just enjoy one another as they navigated the neighborhood.

There were also the long car drives every school day afternoon. Hannah was still registered for school under her biological father's address so that his daughter would not have to switch schools. Both parents reasonably agreed that it would be best for Hannah to finish her schooling amongst the company of her friends. The hormonal devils they knew were already enough of a handful and neither parent could imagine the chaos of inviting ones they didn't know into their impressionable daughters' scholastic sphere.

Five days a week, Daniel spent thirty minutes driving across the county line to pick up Hannah. It was a modest high school, nestled into one of the many smaller satellite communities scattered in a 50-mile radius around Martinsburg. It happened to be just two miles from her father's failing farm, but he rarely could be bothered to pick Hannah up himself.

Despite the traffic and hassle, Daniel enjoyed the drive. It afforded him a scheduled window in which he could just sit back and think. Think about how things were souring between him and Kimberly. About how he seemed to be growing ever closer to Hannah. About his exit strategy, should the circumstances shift in such a way that the only remaining choice was to bail on the failed experiment.

There was almost always time to stop at that last gas station, so sticky and convenient. Daniel usually needed to sneak another pack of cigarettes into his day, an addictive excuse which allowed him the justification of buying Hannah a bottle of her favorite water, overpriced and overhyped. But it was sometimes the small things that build the bigger picture and, judging from Hannah's reaction the first time she climbed into Daniel's passenger side and was greeted with the familiar sight of her favorite candy bar and bottle of water waiting for her, it was easy to tell that not many people had ever gone out of their way for Hannah's benefit.

Daniel always made a special point to sincerely ask about her day at school. He asked more like a friend would, rather than an overly intrusive parental figure. That made it easy for Hannah to talk with Daniel. Especially since he always seemed to remember the names of her friends, and their egregious social offenses, so Hannah did not have to constantly repeat things like she had to when talking with her mother.

They talked their way through most of a school years' worth of mile markers. Not many topics were off limits as Daniel did his best to explain the workings of the world to a precociously receptive teen girl. Romance was a common theme as Hannah dated her way through most of the eligible boys in her class. And some who were ineligible.

The topics of drugs and sex were handled openly and with only a minimal amount of giggled embarrassment. Personal accountability was the rock upon which Daniel tried his best to lay a foundation inside of an unstable seventeen-year-old girl, already threatening to crumble at the first real touch of the adult world. Those awkward high school fingerings paled in comparison to what awaited Hannah in her adulthood. And Daniel wanted her prepared for the inevitable intrusions.

Daniel sometimes shared some of his past with her, carefully filtering out anything inappropriate. Occasionally, when Hannah asked him about his day, the topic turned to writing since Daniel was still struggling his creative best to somehow break into the writing world.

And it wasn't going very well.

Not when Daniel had to play referee between two fighting women, arguing over what seemed, to a more reasonable observer standing uncommittedly on the periphery, ridiculous nonsense. Because everything had to be a disagreement. Every point was crafted in contention. There was no common ground of opinion shared between mother and daughter, leaving an impotently mute boyfriend standing on the sidelines of their many battlefields.

The relationship was breaking under the weight of the collective indifference. Everyone in the house could feel the energy turn toxic, especially on the nights when Daniel was guilted into staying over. Kimberly wanted to keep him close. Daniel just wanted to go back to the comfort of his own place and maybe get some words onto paper. But the way Kimberly tugged at his guilt usually convinced him to stay, even though he would probably end up just sleeping on the couch again.

In the morning after, Daniel would just blame his sleeping location on his insomnia. He didn't have the heart to tell Kimberly that he just couldn't stand laying in the same bed with her anymore. Not after too many nights of suffering lackluster intercourse, only to have her roll immediately over and drift away into a drooling, fart-filled, sleep.

Summer break loomed ahead. Every day became cemented in a pattern that was hastening the collapse of the coupling. Mother and daughter would inevitably get into a fight about something. Each one then tried using their various charms and persuasions to manipulate Daniel into standing on their side. And Daniel was growing tired of having to duck and dodge his way through that disaster of female unpredictability.

It was a Thursday night, bleeding into an early Friday morning, when Hannah caught Daniel. He had patiently waited until he could clearly hear Kimberly's snores over the television before starting to gather up his things. The letter, already typed and painstakingly edited, waited for Kimberly on the kitchen counter, right in front of the coffee maker.

Some might consider that decision as the coward's way out. But Daniel did not see it that way. They never allowed him to get much of a word in while the three of them were home. Individually, he could handle them; together, they were unfixable.

And he was done trying.

Hannah had stayed up well past her suggested bedtime, playing on her phone. She texted friends and wasted time watching pointless videos. It wasn't until well after 1:00 o'clock in the morning when Hannah realized that the familiar clack of Daniels typewriter wasn't echoing through the house.

The first time she had heard it, Hannah hated that typewriter. It was annoyingly penetrative and it distracted her from the dramas unfolding behind a teen girl's closed bedroom door. But then later, once she and Daniel became closer, and he let her read some of his writing, Hannah's opinion changed. The sound of keys striking paper on platen eventually became Hannah's bedtime lullaby.

The silence in the house that too early Friday morning was palpable, compelling Hannah to investigate.

The look on Daniel's face when she surprised him in the kitchen explained everything. The random boxes and bags staged by the garage door, containing most Daniel's personal items, only cemented Hannah's suspicions.

Hannah felt tears in her eyes. Tears that she did not want Daniel to see.

"Are you…" she started, before trailing off.

"Look, Bunny," Daniel began, using a nickname he had given her months before when she was so amped from the day at school that she was literally twitching like a bunny the entire drive home. Hannah initially protested, but the nickname stuck. And Hannah was incensed that he dared call her such a short-fused term of endearment.

"I'm not your Bunny. I'm not even your daughter. You're just the dude who's fucking my mom!" she yelled, before turning away to retreat to the solitary comfort of her locked bedroom.

"It's not like that, Hannah. Wait!" Daniel called out to the disappearing form of a very pissed off girl. But he knew that his words would fail to land.

Hoping that Hannah would one day later in her adulthood better understand the situation, Daniel returned to his silent packing, dejectedly telling himself that it would be better that things end this way.

Before placing his copy of Kimberly's house key on top of the typed note, Daniel dropped the last of his things onto the pile staged to go. He retrieved from the back pocket of his jeans another letter that he had written. A letter that he had written just for Hannah. A letter that broke his heart twice. Once when he was writing it. And then again when he slid that goodbye, so carefully worded, under Hannah's bedroom door.

Hannah barely slept that night. It seemed like an eternity before she heard her mother cursing downstairs in the kitchen. She knew then that her mom had found the letter.

At that moment, Hannah felt herself hating Daniel. Despite all the promises he had made to her, he ended up leaving her, too. Just like all boys do. It had all been lies. Or some elaborate scheme to get her mother into bed, only to dump her the second he got his nostalgic rocks off.

Hanna wanted Daniel to hurt as badly as she was hurting. Despite everything, she didn't want her mom upset. Not like that, anyway. Hannah got revenge for both of them when she walked into the kitchen and uttered four simple words: "Mama? He touched me."

That one lie gave Kimberly perfect justification for having to kick to the curb the man who had hurt her daughter, in Kimberly's revised timeline of events. It would help take the sting and embarrassment out of their mutual abandonment, holding Daniel responsible for the abuses that never really happened.

Of course, that was not the story that Hannah shared with her mom that first morning. The story she later repeated to the investigating officers of the Martinsburg Police Department who had been assigned to Hannah's case. That story was full of sordid details outlining the many ways in which Daniel had supposedly taken advantage of her.

All the research Hannah had explored online as she waited for her mom to awaken paid off brilliantly as she explained positions she had never actually experienced. The officers took diligent notes, mentally tallying up the felonies as they scribbled in their notebooks.

Daniel was arrested the next morning, when the early summer Martinsburg Saturday still held some promise of being a decent day. At least until the squad cars came screeching into the scene.

Handcuffs. Pat downs. Miranda warning. A few random mutterings of "You sick pedo fuck." Downtown processing. Fingerprinting. Electronic photographs taken and filed away. Those hours were just a blur for Daniel as he sat in an interview room, waiting for the questions to start.

At first, Daniel mistakenly thought that perhaps Kimberly, in a fit of breakup rage, might have filed a domestic complaint against him. He certainly would not put it past her to stoop so low as to file a false accusation of abuse with the Martinsburg Police Department. It wasn't until the investigating officer began peppering his inquisitions with mentions of Hannah that Daniel was able to contextually piece together what was happening. And once he had made that connection, Daniel's heart sank.

It sank not because of the betrayal. Or because of the laborious prospect ahead of him of fighting to clear his name. It sank because Daniel knew that the moment the accusations had left Hanna's mouth, his life was effectively over.

Even if he were to clear his name, and walk away an innocent man in the eyes of the law, Daniel knew that the eyes of the community would see it differently. He was damaged goods. And there was no bouncing back from that accusation once it stuck.

Thankfully, Daniels' public defender provided him with a respectable representation. That, coupled with a near total lack of physical evidence- the rape kit had come back negative- allowed for Daniel to be released on a significant bail that he could just barely afford.

The stigma followed Daniel through his day. Everywhere he went in Martinsburg he seemed to be attracting stares and whispers. It felt like he was walking through town with a target on his chest, the modern-day interpretation of letters that used to be scarlet.

Daniel lost his job when his employers found out. His landlord was also threatening to evict him, just as soon as he could find a legal justification for doing so. His neighbors pointed at him, mockingly. Mothers swiftly redirected their children in stores and on sidewalks.

The weight of that undeserved mark became too much for Daniel to bear. It broke his soul that people could really see him committing those accused atrocities. It killed his spirit when he witnessed his name being slanderously posted to websites. Googling his name destroyed his future. Beyond an oddly placed link to a social media page, most of the results described his arrest and the accusations made against him.

The late afternoon Indiana sunshine illuminated Daniel's desk as he sat and typed out his letters. The one for his family, sent care of a dependable sister out in Colorado. The letter to his attorney, thanking him for his services and asking an unconventional favor. The third letter, brief and heart-wrenching, Daniel wrote to Hannah.

A last tidying of his manuscripts, left neatly arranged on the crooked table by the door. One final beer, because Daniel's mouth was dry. That last cigarette, deliciously soothing in its smoldering finality. One final playing of his favorite song, the last mix-tape entry on the playlist of Daniel's life.

He thought that the room felt oddly cold.

Daniel waited for the closing notes of the song to echo through his living room before committing to that tug of a trigger's lasting pull.

III

Neither Kimberly, nor Hannah, attended Daniel's memorial service. In fact, it was a sparsely attended affair considering how awful the accusations against Daniel had been and which had captivated both the press and the invasive Martinsburg social grape vines. His suicide only seemed to escalate the whispers of guilt and disdain for the city's newest fallen son- everybody loves watching a falling star.

But there was one person in Martinsburg who knew the truth. And Hannah was struggling to live with the weight of that lie.

Her acting out was initially excused as a lingering side effect from the sexual assaults. The shoplifting, too. And, the fights, fought both electronically and physically at the mall.

Through it all, all the counseling sessions and all the time spent in back security offices waiting for her mom to show up to try and get Hannah released from another shoplifting charge, Hannah knew the truth.

And she thought about it often.

She knew that Daniel really did love, and care, about her. Of that there was never any doubt. And though they often did not necessarily agree on everything, Daniel always treated her with a respect now absent in her life.

Hannah had something beautiful and she tossed it away in the heat of one bad decision. Daniel had been more of a father to Hannah than her biological creator had ever been and Hannah missed that affection. Just because she sometimes rebelled against it didn't mean that Hannah didn't subconsciously realize just how desperately she needed that guidance in her life.

Those feelings were only reinforced the day a letter arrived at the house, large and legal looking. Hannah had stayed home from school, under the guise of a fake panic attack. It allowed her to be the first one with access to that day's mail delivery.

Hannah had been hoping to intercept the notification from school that she was getting suspended. Instead, Hannah stumbled into something else.

The large letter was addressed to her, sent care of her mom. Since her name was on it, Hannah didn't feel too guilty surrendering to her curiosity and ripping it open.

There was a top letter, from Daniel's attorney, explaining the contents and context of the other letter inside. The letter from Daniel. That he had written the day he died. The letter he had written for Hannah.

Normally, such a letter probably wouldn't be sent. But Daniel's lawyer, fully convinced of his client's innocence, decided that final wish of an innocent dead man should be respected. And he followed through on that wish.

Hannah, fearful of what the smaller envelope might contain, retreated to the security of her room. She sat on her bed, cluttered with clothes, and opened the letter.

She began crying almost instantly; Hannah did not realize just how much she had missed being called Bunny:

"Bunny,

I will never understand why you said the things that you did. You know that I never hurt you like that.

But, I am choosing to forgive you. Not because I really want to. But because I cannot allow myself to be angry. Not now.

I much prefer that my last thought be a happy one.

Please, take care of yourself. And know that I will always love you like you were my own. Because in my heart, you always were.

Be kind. Be happy. And have a kick ass life, kid.

I will love you, always.

-- Daniel"

Hannah continued to cry. She knew that she had made a terrible mistake.

She had taken away her one positive male role model in a sea of defectively selfish impostors. She had robbed herself of the person who took the time to genuinely understand her. She had left herself a daddy's girl in a world without a daddy.

And it broke her heart.

Because she was tired of the exhausting lies. She was tired of carrying the burden of being a falsified victim. She was disgusted with always being translucent, her person replaced indelibly by the repercussions of her dishonesty.

Hannah looked to the one role model she had ever had and retrieved from her mother's closet Daniel's typewriter. It was the one thing of his that Kimberly had salvaged from that pile at the edge of the street.

It took her some trial and error. But having spent some time secretly watching Daniel as he wrote, Hannah eventually figured out the technological nuances involved in using his old machine.

Hannah sat on her bed, cross-legged, and methodically began typing out a letter of her own.

Martinsburg Daily Herald
Sunday, October 23, 2016

A Celebration of Life in honor of Hannah Jean McCleary, 17, is scheduled for Wednesday, 5-8 p.m. Participants strongly encouraged to wear purple, Hanna's favorite color.

In lieu of flowers, the family requests donations be made to either the Martinsburg Suicide Hotline, or the Martinsburg S.P.C.A.

"When I'm feeling weak
and my pain walks down a one-way street,
I look above
and I know I'll always be blessed with love"

-Robbie Williams, "Angels"

Rabbit Holes

"Seriously?"

The day had not started well for Christian Pierce. Punctuating that point, an official-looking "WEED NOTICE VIOLATION" sign had been staked into the scraggle of overgrown grass that apparently the City of Martinsburg, Indiana, legally considered his front yard. It was barely more than a park strip, just large enough to foster the encroachment of invasive weeds.

Christian had moved into the dilapidated house only a few short months previously after his former girlfriend mustered up her courage and shoved him out to that very literal curb. It was only after weeks of pawning, stealing, and scamming that Christian finally secured the funds to pay the deposit and the first month's rent on a fresh start.

With no one even moderately responsible around to supervise him, Christian fell into the cathartic grip of a dirt-bag bender, epic in its level of indecency. Clear alcohols throbbed through scabby veins, aching to feel something different. And on that hot July morning, Christian was feeling brutally hungover.

He knew that soon the morning ritual of bile-splattering purging would start. There was no option but to peel himself off a dirty sheet, stained rigid from too many spills and too many purgatorial nights spent in a sweat-soaked, bed-wetting hell, and begin searching for anything that might delay what was inevitably coming right back up.

When his world seemed more definitive, Christian pinballed down the narrow corridor leading into a musty kitchen. He wanted to invite some caffeine into his morning ritual because not only did it help get the stagnant blood moving quicker, it also pushed the other substances to higher levels of effectiveness.

The frowstiness of the house forced Christian to seek out cleaner breaths by relocating to the front stoop, once the coffee had finished splashing into a stained mug. The claustrophobic fear was twinging inside of him and Christian just wasn't in the mood for any of that shit.

Mug precariously in shaking hand, and a crumpled cigarette dangling limply from chapped and peeling lips, Christian stepped onto his front porch. He was immediately hit with a humid wall of an Indiana summer heatwave punching him in the face. The dense air made it difficult for Christian to catch his smoker's breath, leaving him gasping at the filtered tip of his cigarette.

It was then that he saw the sign mocking his apparent lack of landscaping skills.

"Those assholes."

The yard wasn't that bad in his opinion. That summer had been far too hot and dry for any real grass to grow. But knowing from experience that you just can't fight any uniformed representative of City Hall, Christian accepted that he would have to mow sometime in the next five days. If he didn't, then hired strangers would roll in like some lawn care S.W.A.T. team, mow sloppily, and bill his scummy landlord for the inflated expenses.

Christian finished his coffee and cigarette just as quickly as the intolerable Indiana weather would allow and disappeared back inside. He had to prepare himself for the discomfort of completing the adult task of keeping his lawn nice and tidy during a blistering Midwestern heatwave while hellishly hungover. Christian took a moment to rub his eyes before heading to the dilapidated garage out back. There was only a small window of time in which to gas up the mower and get the damn lawn mowed before the Indiana sun became too blazingly oppressive.

Surprisingly, there was still some gas in the scrounged can. Christian couldn't remember the details of just how he had acquired either it, or the mower. There were only fuzzy recollections of a late-night, side-alley metal grab, back when Christian was forced to scavenge scrap to later hustle into more recreational substances.

Christian tackled the easy front part of his lawn first and not just because it was the most visible. He instead was hoping to catch the attentions of some random passing girl, impressing her with his pale skin glistening from the sweat that started the moment he pulled himself from his bed.

With the front finished, and no unreasonably willing girls having passed him by, Christian maneuvered the still running mower through the narrow and mostly dysfunctional side gate leading to the back yard. Stopping only long enough for a couple of bumps through carnival glass, Christian felt his brain shift into a more familiar gear.

Christian began mowing along a fence that offered a disappointing amount of privacy. The mower clogged constantly at the influx of weeds, causing Christian to repeatedly push the mower handle down, popping the front wheels up to give the struggling blades a chance to catch up.

The fourth time the mower fell back level with the ground, Christian heard a sound not normally associated with yardwork. It was a little too piercing and the different vibrations signified that something other than a weed, or stump, had met the dull blades of his sputtering mower. The screech echoing off the battered boards of the fence was also a clear indicator that something was amiss.

Pulling the mower back to investigate, Christian discovered what had caused the unexpected sounds and vibrations. He had accidentally set the running machine down on top of an unseen, and slightly underdeveloped, rabbit.

Angered at the pointless stupidity of the situation, Christian gazed unaffected upon the remains of what had, only a few seconds before, constituted a healthy, and fully intact, innocent creature.

He shrugged his shoulders at the sight of the small, mutilated corpse. How did it not hear the mower coming closer? Why did it not try and hop away to the safety of another part of the yard?

"Hakuna matata," Christian snickered to no one, as he reached down to give the starter rope a swift tug before the engine cooled off too much. When the mower sprang back into life, he side-stepped the bloody remnants and continued mowing until the yard was presentable enough to pass muster when next the Weed Cops came prowling.

The rest of that day was the usual blur, fueled mainly by an ill-advised expedition to the local corner store to stock up on conveniently bottled bad decisions, embarrassingly purchased with fists full of sticky change. The rainbow of pharmaceuticals contributed for as long as Christian maintained some semblance of consciousness. But when he crossed the threshold of his tolerance, the dreams started.

Unlike the carnage of an unforgiving reality, the rabbit in his dreams had only lost a single ear in the accident. While not a life-threatening injury, it still unsettled Christian as he unconsciously navigated through another sweaty night of tossing and turning at the tortured cinematic projections of his imagination.

Upon waking, to both the memory of an accidental kill, and a new nasty voicemail informing him that he had been fired from yet another shit-level dishwashing job, Christian accepted that it was going to be one of those days.

"Fuck."

Christian took comfort in knowing that he had survived being unemployed before. In the grand, universal sense, this newest job loss really wasn't that big of a deal; he knew that he could get by. Even if he had to start slinging baggies again. Or pleasing those random shadows for ready cash, down along the railroad tracks that surgically divide Martinsburg into the "haves" and the "don't give a shits." And the first step of surviving a recently expected unemployment was to get as numb as was addictively possible, then to stay that way for as long as the dwindling funds hold out.

Christian did exactly that, successfully suffering another oppressive Martinsburg summer day, watching with unfocusing eyes as the light gradually crept over the city before transitioning back into darkness. Not that the approaching evening hours slowed Christian's consumption. In fact, the invading night only caused him to begin ingesting at an alarmingly unsafe rate. Memories of that damn rabbit had contaminated his thoughts and Christian found himself facing a familiar fear that was pushing him to stay awake- if he was awake, he could not dream. If he did not dream, he would not have to suffer.

Eventually, Christian's body could no longer hold out against the influx of bad decisions and slipped over to the other side where the rabbit was ready to greet him.

When the rabbit appeared out of the bushes in his dream, both ears were missing from two bloody stumps where thick blood pumped out every time the rabbit moved. It left a trail across the imagined grass of a backyard better tended than in reality. But something was different inside the confines of that dream. And though outrageously altered, Christian's body instinctively tucked itself into the familiar safety of a fetal position on his stained bed.

He could feel a presence standing near the wounded rabbit, scurrying around in the grass. Leaning against the warped boards of the privacy fence was the fuzzy outline of Christian's younger brother, Andrew. The little brother, born deaf, who died young because he could not hear the car careening around the curve by their childhood house when Christian threw that football, intentionally leading little Andrew out into the street.

Flashes of his older brother cruelty tormented Christian, filling his mind with regret at just how awfully he had abused his younger sibling all through Andrew's brief, and silent, childhood.

When Christian opened his eyes, he was immediately hit with a rush of remorse that he knew he would have to drink back down. That became the pattern into which Christian fell because the dreams kept getting worse. The voices were shouting louder. He had to find a way to block it all out.

And he did...at least until the curtain of exhaustion enveloped him.

The rabbit, in addition to its ears, was now losing limbs. The right rear leg was missing, leaving a weeping stump twitching horribly every time the rabbit attempted to hop. And, like the night before, a new presence had joined the figure of his brother Andrew along the fence.

The taller outline of his uncle leaned against that of his long-dead baby brother. His one-legged Uncle. The Uncle who had left part of himself in a foreign country when he was barely a man, struggling to survive a drafted tour of Southeast Asia. The Uncle he was sporadically forced to visit in any number of State mental hospitals through much of Christian's childhood years, at least before that uncle achieved final success during one of his numerous attempts.

Christian could smell his uncle's unfiltered cigarettes and the beer on his breath. He watched as the figures of his deceased relatives seemed to engage themselves in conversation, occasionally pointing towards him, snickering.

When Christian awoke from the newest horrors, the best that he could manage was muttering "What the fuck was that?" before starting the whole cycle over again. He tried his best to ignore the implications; he tried rationalizing his way through it. But Christian still caught himself looking out the grimy kitchen window, the one facing the backyard, terrified that he might catch a glimpse of what he had already witnessed.

He realized that if he was to survive this madness, he would have to significantly change his game. Christian forced himself out into the tick-tock rhythms of a punishing Martinsburg summer day, seeking out sketchy people to make even sketchier deals. Forsaking the usually soothing comforts of his usual appetites, Christian instead pursued more aggressively stimulating players with which to arm himself.

Drained by the day's hunt and subsequent consumption, Christian's plan crumbled predictably as he transitioned into the temporary dark. It did not take long for the rabbit to appear and the escalation of injuries was substantial.

Even though now both of its hind legs were missing, the rabbit still attempted to hop closer to Christian. It was whining. The voices from the fence were laughing louder. And a new voice had joined those of Christian's little brother and Uncle. A voice that forced an involuntary whimper from Christian, deeply caught in his R.E.M. spin-cycle unconsciousness.

It was the gruff voice of Christian's grandfather.

The grandfather who opened a typewriter repair shop after returning from the war. And then made Christian touch him in those weird ways in its stale backroom office. Touches that occurred far too frequently in the chaotic days of Christian's penetrative youth, when his mom would callously abandon him at the shop before going out to chase temporary touches of her own.

The smell of poorly cleaned dentures and machine oil permeated Christian's dream. He relived the taste. And the smells. And the embarrassingly painful sensation of tender flesh tearing.

The rabbit, despite appearing to be in agony from recent amputation of healthy limbs, seemed to be mocking Christian. His long-dead family members provided a background soundtrack, the combined symphony of their laughters jarring Christian awake into the undesirable embrace of another blurred day filled with the same crippling obstructions.

There are, after all, only so many dead relatives that one person can reasonably tolerate before things start truly falling apart.

More days injected with drug-fueled insanity and over-indulgence. More nights pierced with imagined blood on the butcherblock of Christian's dreams. More voices, screaming and murmuring and laughing.

Fueled on by an uppers-driven mania, Christian barricaded himself in a room filled with empty bottles, overflowing ashtrays, and the lingering haze of smoke left from a stream of constantly consumed cheap tobacco. In the background, a record player, skipping and jumping at the end of its final groove, added a scratchy anthem to the room. In that atmosphere of palpable despair, Christian sought his tangible release.

He retrieved a typewriter from the back of a seldom used closet and removed a scratched machine from a musty case. That olfactory splinter triggered Christian right back to that horrid office where he had been forced to surrender his innocence.

The dim light cast from a lamp with its torn shade askew highlighted haphazardly stacked papers. He had filled them with the typed gibberish of a man in the final stages of collapse. Christian raged mechanically on the glass-topped keys, spending hysterical hours typing out a rambling manifesto that no one would ever read. He found himself documenting circumstances beyond comprehension, forcing the gamble of capturing his fallibility on paper. Because maybe then, Christian would finally be able to understand it.

Overwhelmed, Christian felt himself surrendering to another terrifying twilight's dark kiss.

The rabbit chose that moment to exert more of its grim influence.

The ears- long gone and missing. As were all the rabbit's other appendages. Christian was horrified to see that the skin had been peeled away, leaving nothing but twitching, exposed musculature. And that tragic torso of quivering flesh was straining to hold Christian somehow accountable.

The rabbit struggled, screaming and bleeding.

Gnawing and dying.

Christian understood, even in the deepest unpredictability of his dream, what must be done. No creature deserves a fate like that poor rabbit was experiencing, as it pathetically tried crawling across Christian's yard on legs that just were not there.

The ethereal outlines of his deceased relatives continued to tease and point at Christian from the periphery. But he no longer cared. Maybe if he took matters into his own hands, and ended that rabbit's suffering, perhaps his madness would finally stop, too.

Christian knelt in front of the rabbit. He reached out and took the bloody, skinless form into his hands.

It felt warm and uncomfortably sticky.

Against the tension of a bent knee, Christian made the twist.

A sound, sharp and specific, echoed out through his unconsciousness.

The screaming stopped; his dead relatives remained still.

There was a calming silence echoing inside of Christian's head for a few refreshing seconds.

A mechanical whooshing sound shattered the quiet.

The first touch of a gentle rush of air against Christian's face chilled the sweat glistening on his brow.

Through the hazy, nonsensical parameters of his mania, Christian's gaze instinctively looked up. A large spinning blade, growing more menacingly deadly as it rapidly descended, was approaching with alarming speed.

There wasn't even time enough to scream.

Martinsburg Daily Herald
August 26, 2015

Local Martinsburg resident Christian Pierce, 36, was found deceased in his home yesterday afternoon, the victim of a tragic home accident. Authorities confirmed that an improperly installed ceiling fan had shaken free and fell upon Pierce as he slept, killing him. Autopsy and toxicology reports are pending. The Martinsburg Police currently do not suspect foul play.

Hoosier Crossroads

I

"I've been looking forward to this," Trevor said to himself, as dirty, calloused fingers opened the somewhat chilled "tall boy" stashed inside an extra work sweatshirt before his shift had even started. It was honestly the only reason he kept that company embroidered garment inside his Jeep. The temperatures inside the steel production facility seldom cooled enough to ever warrant having to wear a sweatshirt.

That Monday shift at Garter Steel was the usual shit-show of conflicting instructions, mismanaged line changeovers, and the expected level of Midwestern union-backed mediocrity. It had taken some fifteen years before Trevor was able to finally secure one of the better shifts the company offered, the second shift running Monday through Thursday, 2 p.m. to midnight. And all it cost him was the selling of his soul to the Steel Workers Union.

Four days a week, forty-nine weeks out of the year, Trevor Bedford disappeared inside the sprawling Garter Steel complex, expanding out north of Woltonville, Indiana. A few more miles down the road and he would have had to cross the Illinois state line, but instead, the company had settled in Indiana, clinging tenaciously to the tax brackets offered by the state. It was a last-ditch effort by all parties involved to find a way of staying economically relevant in the modern manufacturing era, while all around the region the once thriving "Rust Belt" continued rusting away in the imported onslaught of cheap Chinese steel.

The job had originally offered a young Martinsburg couple a steady sense of financial stability after Trevor Bedford and Angie Wright exchanged their wedding vows the year they both turned nineteen. They felt fortunately comfortable and it wasn't long before new additions were made to the family. First their son, Ryan, joined them. Krystal, their daughter, followed a few years later.

Trevor loved both of his children equally and he tried his exhausted best to provide a guiding influence. But it all started falling apart with the terrible arguments fought regarding what they should name their unborn daughter.

Trevor fought for his baby girl to be christened with a more traditional name, a position reinforced by his observations of Angie's obvious lack of mature parenting skills. In his mind, naming their beautiful baby girl Krystal would only condemn his daughter to a future earned by swinging her ass on brightly polished poles.

Trevor lost that battle and something about the significance of that defeat made shut him down inside. Maybe it was the unfairness with which his wife fought. Maybe it was the childish mind games, fraught with the stinging insults and the constant withholding of intimacy that got him down. But something inside of Trevor died in the passive-aggressive manipulations.

Losing himself in his job four days a week- and overtime whenever he could score it- was about the only escape left open to him. That, and Trevor's increasing alcohol consumption, barely noticed by anyone who mattered, despite the recyclable evidence hidden around the house.

While Trevor found himself trapped by the responsibility of providing for his young family, and the bottles that secretly supported that effort, Angie began pursuing being a stay-at-home cheat.

After her short-lived dream of becoming a children's book author failed miserably, Angie found herself starving for validation from any available man who was unlucky enough to enter the orbital tugs of her P.T.A. helicoptering motherhood seductions. Through almost the entirety of the couple's little cookie cutter subdivision she spread the wet resume of her desperate sex, in the well-lubed hopes of finding a more materialistically satisfying partner.

The stories Angie submitted for publication were like her actual day to day life- not that interesting. And Trevor eventually grew into rejecting her stories, too. It was an easy stance to take once he learned the full extent of her
indiscretions, leading him to immediately sue for both divorce and full custody of the children.

The battle of separation was protracted and grueling. Angie relied on her invented victim status to avail herself of numerous programs intended to help women truly in need, stealing resources from those who truly needed it the most. It was the only way to feed her narcissism and to pay her mounting legal bills.

In order to present the best possible petition, Trevor cashed in his retirement fund and lawyered up with the best legal counsel he could afford. To him, and his concept of parenting, that was just something a dad is supposed to do- fight tirelessly for the sake of his kids. Had he known how unfairly the deck was stacked against him, however, Trevor would have been better off hiding his money.

For quite some time, ever since the societal tolerance for divorce has sifted over into a grudging acceptance, too many family courts have been polluted with false notions of biological capabilities and have rendered their verdicts with a sexist slant. Far too often the courts habitually side with the mother on questions of custody based solely on the fact they gave birth and therefore, must be the better parent.

It did not matter that Angie was verbally and mentally abusive towards the children, accusations which Trevor had overwhelming evidence to support. The court did not care that she never held an actual job in her life, resulting in no financial or housing stability for the kids. She even had a brief police record, back from when she was gently shoplifting in order to chase a desperately needed high before that compulsion to be fulfilled was ultimately transformed into the hunt for new suburban dick.

Trevor had never been arrested. And, despite Angie's many projected accusations, he never once cheated. On her, or anyone else. He had responsibly held the same job for fifteen years and was never once late on a single house payment.

But sadly, in the eyes of a sexist court that is supposed to be blind in its judgements, Trevor was found lacking before even stepping foot inside the courtroom simply by virtue of being a father.

Their final divorce decree clearly illustrated that Midwestern, God-fearing inequity.

While granted the divorce, Trevor was only allocated a single weekend a month of custody. And the level of child support he was also ordered to pay was quite staggering- extinguishing any hopes of comfortable retirement.

The worst aspect to all the hearings, and meetings, and mediations, was that by ruling in her favor, the judge validated all of Angie's lies and manipulations. It stamped her ticket for a free ride and Angie was going to milk that opportunity for all it was worth, sucking hard until the rewarding money shot came, just as she had learned to do from her revolving door parade of cul-de-sac penises.

That court-mandated empowerment fed the flames of her burning resentment and it turned Angie into the cliché crazy ex. It pushed her to insult and belittle Trevor, often in front of the kids, something which he never did. She took every opportunity to seek an increase in the child support payments, even though he was already paying substantially to help provide for his kids. And very little of that money actually trickled down to them, being spent instead of manicures, designer clothes, and "wine weekends" away with the girls.

It was starting to tear Trevor down.

Losing his kids hurt. Deeply. Having to move out of the house she was awarded in the divorce and into a more modest place, halfway between Martinsburg and Woltonville, stung. Watching his kids polluted and poisoned against him in the storms of Angie's raging instabilities, broke him.

Trevor's life became a stale maze of blandness. He simply shut off his heart, went to work, and drank away the hours between shifts.

The little farmhouse he rented offered some buffer from the insanity because it spared Trevor the possibility of ever randomly bumping into Angie around town. He didn't have neighbors right at his property line like he had before, so it was beneficial to his need for isolation. And, it was only a 25-minute commute to Grater Steel if he took the interstate, though he seldom ever chose that route.

Trevor preferred the safe solitude provided by the back-country roads, allowing him the opportunity to get a head start on his drinking. The back-route commute also had the benefit of providing the promise of better scenery, the interstate only offering predictably bland billboards and obnoxious SUVs crowding the lanes. And for some reason, Trevor occasionally enjoyed driving by that small, gated cemetery, just on the south side of Woltonville.

The aging, somewhat neglected cemetery sits catty-corner from an annoyingly inconvenient four-way stop, marked at the bottom of a gentle slope in the Hoosier farmland. The crooked and rusting wrought iron cemetery fence is bordered by farm fields filled with crops that rotate depending on the season, and the flush and virginal woods lining the currents of a Stone River flowing down to Martinsburg.

He could never figure out the reasons why, but Trevor noticed that regardless of which direction he approached the cemetery, the radio in his Jeep always fuzzed out. Trevor just attributed the temporary musical blackout to some quirk in the topography and considered the annoyance as just part of the trip.

Trevor had almost finished his illegally consumed beer when he abruptly rolled up to the four-way stop. Not seeing the glow of any accusatory headlights approaching, Trevor put his jeep in PARK and hopped out the door into the warm Indiana summer night.

He really needed to piss.

Jumping across the small ditch running alongside the county road, Trevor landed with a thump on the cemetery grounds. The light shining out from the open jeep door reflected intimately off the headstones. The sound of crickets and frogs and cicadas married together in the symphony of another warm Midwestern summer night. Behind him, the static from the radio crackled and popped.

Selecting a stone to serve as a surrogate urinal, Trevor unzipped his grungy work jeans with his right hand, still holding the beer can in his left. Fishing around, he finally freed his sweaty, disinterested manhood and began emptying his bladder.

A heavy sigh of physical relief echoed out through the quiet of the cemetery, briefly drowning out the sound of hot urine splashing off carved granite.

While still relieving himself, Trevor tossed back the last of his beer. Satisfied that another soldier had fallen valiantly in the war for his inebriation, Trevor let out a celebratory belch.

A can, skeletal and unnecessary, was thrown into the blackness. The sound of metal bouncing off stone pinged back sharply.

A few shakes, a quick zip, and Trevor was ready to return to his drive. He never was a very superstitious sort of person, so it wasn't some underlying feeling of insecurity or fear of being in a cemetery in the middle of the night that was egging him to hurry. It was the promise of another bottle calling him from across the miles.

Trevor reached into his pocket and pulled a cigarette from its pack.

A quick lighter's flick and the immediate surroundings were illuminated surprisingly bright for such a small flame.

He exhaled that first heavy lungful of smoke.

"You lucky motherfuckers," he mumbled to no stone, while shaking his head at the rows of headstones barely visible in the inky blackness of a back-country Hoosier night.

A quick hop over the drainage ditch and Trevor settled in the driver's seat.

The instant he shifted the jeep from PARK into drive, the radio crackled back into life.

"That's weird," Trevor said to no one in particular.

Shrugging his shoulders at the unexpected electronic inconsistencies, the Jeep accelerated though the four-way stop.

As the red glow of taillights disappeared into a moonless Indiana summer night, the faint sounds of Trevor singing along to AD/DC's "Highway to Hell" hung in the humid air.

II

Tuesday proved to be a west central Indiana carbon copy of the day before and the summer weather greeting Trevor when he opened his eyes threatened to be clear and hot. In his hungover state, he would have preferred cool and cloudy to help muffle the world and to allow his body time to process the many self-ingested poisons still coursing their way through his system. But on that particular Tuesday, Trevor was not fortunate enough to have mother nature on his side.

The smell of stale smoke, earthy and rank, drifted through the small farmhouse as Trevor prepared for another soul-roasting shift at Grater Steel. There was little comfort to the brutal regularity of his routine, the dial tone dance Trevor danced dutifully, four days a week.

The day's first smoke, sparked while pissing off the back deck because it was closer than the bathroom and less claustrophobic, was the beginning of Trevor's morning ritual. Opening a "wake up" beer to keep him company in his shower was next.

After making himself presentable enough to be in the company of other steel workers, Trevor gathered the items necessary for surviving another day with an indelible blue stained into his collar. In addition to his phone, wallet, keys, and ID badge, Trevor slipped a small green bottle into the daily mix, just to give himself a little treat after suffering through his shift.

The drive to Grater Steel was uneventful and Trevor's shift as Stove Tender was free of both accident and error, always considered a win in such a high stake, coal-fueled manufacturing landscape.

A summer evening, cool and clear, greeted Trevor as he navigated the maze of the Grater Steel Employee Parking Lot. He sat in his Jeep, smoking the first of his many post-shift cigarettes while waiting for his co-workers to finish the nightly scramble for the exit.

When he finally turned out of the parking lot, onto the patched asphalt of Indiana State Route 36, Trevor finally began to relax. Deep pulls, in rapid succession from the green bottle retrieved from his trusty sweatshirt, helped significantly.

As he ground out the miles towards home, Trevor let his mind wander. He began thinking of random injustices and occurrences, dwelling on situations and conversations, long since resolved, but still somehow lingering inside his head.

He thought about his boy and wondered what kind of man he would grow to be under his mother's twisted tutelage. He questioned whether he should begin the fight for more custody as his daughter was growing into a sexually-charged adolescence. It terrified Trevor to think Krystal would base her development on her mother's fleshy and ill-advised influence.

Trevor figured that it was even odds he would be a grandfather by the time he reached forty. And that thought festered.

The pain he began experiencing in his gut had nothing to do with the bottom shelf Irish pushed into an empty, post-shift stomach. He'd played that game too many times before for his body to now be in shocked revolt. It was all those thoughts of parenting mistakes, both his and his ex-wife's, that was twisting Trevor's gut.

Thankfully, the four-way stop wasn't too far down State Route 36. Assuming there was no interference to complicate, Trevor knew how he could make things a bit more bearable.

Just as it always did, the radio in the Jeep fizzled out right before the cemetery. It slightly irritated Trevor because it cut off one of his favorite songs. But, having learned through the grueling and emasculating grinder of his divorce not to fight pointlessly against things that he was powerless to change, Trevor ignored the fresh static's crackle.

Luckily, the cross-road stop was devoid of any other traffic. One last scan for interloping headlights and Trevor tossed the Jeep in park and began digging in the center console for his emergency stash.

Tucked within the folds of an owner's manual never read, Trevor retrieved a slightly crumpled, but still smokable, pinner rolled and tucked away the last time he invested in some California chronic.

He avoided smoking pot every day, having had enough of that nonsense throughout his high school years. Once he was married, and a father, Trevor knew that he had to be more cautious. But occasionally, especially when his stomach was trying its best to punch a way outside his skin, Trevor sought the soothing sanctuary of sparking one up. It calmed nerves and lightened the load and he knew that tonight, he was going to need that extra help.

Flicking the butt of his cigarette out the Jeep window with sufficient force that it smacked itself out against one of the headstones closest to the road, Trevor watched it fly. The red-hot cherry arched through the black. It projected a certain beauty, until smattering out in a small shower of burning tobacco scraps.

Another scan for headlights, just for safety.

A metallic flick of a lighter's knurled wheel.

The pungent aroma of marijuana, musty and familiar, filled the Jeep at Trevor's first exhale.

He used his elbow to nudge the lid of the console and it closed with a plastic thunk. At the very same instant the radio sparked into life, filling the cab with unexpected music.

And it was just Trevor's luck that The Police decided to inexplicably show up.

He continued to sit idle at that little four-way stop nestled mostly unnoticed in the Indiana countryside, smoking away his worries and singing along to an unexpected song:

"Every move you make, every step you take, I'll be watching you."

Outside his window, before the song had finished, Trevor could have sworn he saw something moving behind one of the headstones.

He took a deep hit, reminded himself that sometimes pot makes him a little paranoid, and put his Jeep into DRIVE.

III

Wednesday afternoon dawned hard and abrupt for Trevor Bedford.

There were foggy, uncertain memories of the night before polluting his brain the moment red and irritated eyes blinked open.

Trevor hadn't planned on drinking quite so much. Normally he moderated his midweek consumption, fully aware that his work week was not yet at an end. It did not help his attempts at moderation that the strange feeling Trevor felt listening to the radio the night before had followed him all the way home. And it took nearly all that second bottle to finally muffle it out of his head.

He slowly, and awkwardly, stumbled through the well-practiced routine of another work day starting, chalking up the strange new feelings to how much he had smoked, and how little he had eaten, the day before.

Wednesday was another predictably mundane shift at Grater Steel, allowing Trevor to coast by on autopilot. Not wishing to experience a repeat of the day before, he even made a concerted effort to eat something on his breaks and to stay hydrated throughout his shift.

When Trevor finally punched out at the end of his dreary day, he made his way to his waiting Jeep.

Sitting there, alone and waiting for the post-shift traffic to clear the lot, Trevor felt almost nervous about his drive home. So strange was the feeling that he briefly considered taking the interstate home, just to get him home as quickly as possible.

A friendly honk from one of the last cars leaving the lot shook Trevor from his thoughts. He was making a big deal out of literally nothing, he told himself, reassuringly.

"Just get home and it'll be fine," he said to himself, as he reached to turn the ignition over.

With Grater Steel comfortably behind his tires, and the four-way stop looming up ahead, Trevor refrained from reaching for the liquid comfort of his "going home" bottle. The only addictive solace he allowed himself was to smoke a constant chain of cigarettes.

He did not plan to stop to take a leak. The thought of getting high there again sounded like a ridiculously bad idea. Trevor was going to roll through the intersection as quickly as possible and get the hell home.

It was coming up quick. The headlights from the Jeep illuminated the warning signs of the stop ahead. The gentle slope of the road shifted down. Headstones twinkled sporadically in unstable beams of inconsistent light.

The usually welcoming Hoosier farmland suddenly felt unnatural and wrong.

The radio hissing and sputtering static only added to the unease.

Trevor did not expect to hear Bonny Taylor singing out at him when the unpredictable signals stuck:

"Turn around! Every now and then I get a little bit nervous that the best of all the years have gone by..."

IV

Another night drinking.

Another night filled with thoughts about weird feelings on a strange drive home.

Another day born in the murky, hesitant coughs of a pounding hangover lingering far beyond what could ever be considered reasonable.

Trevor was nearing his mental breaking point- suffering the burden of carrying a well-paying, benefit-backed dead-end job. Of trying to be a decent father to two kids who constantly belittled and ignored him. Ignoring the muted warnings of addictions spiraling out of control in ever-increasing, "on the way home" doses.

His body hurt. His brain felt pickled. But Trevor still managed to get himself to work on time. All through that Thursday shift, which was Trevor's Friday, he suffered through the normally mundane and pointless chatter of his co-workers. And today, the herd mentality at Grater Steel became stuck on a topic that had a direct bearing on the upcoming weekend.

The long-awaited lane expansion of the interstate feeding that part of Indiana had finally begun, complicating the commute for most of the workers in the area. On lunch breaks, and in cubicled offices, and the parking lot, a cacophony of complaints and jokes and swear words resonated out in fruitless criticisms about the anticipated delays.

Trevor could only shake his head at the newest dose of bad luck unexpectedly injected into an already unlucky existence.

Rarely did he travel the interstate himself, inadvertently distancing himself from the signs posted weeks ago. Thanks to the over-zealous Department of Transportation of the state of Indiana, he would have to rely on his usual back country road route to get him safely home after work, instead of shooting down the interstate like he had uncharacteristically decided on the drive in that gloomy and damp Thursday.

Eventually, the drudgery of the week's last second shift came to an end and the grungy crowd of exhausted steel workers spilled out loudly into the parking lot.

Trevor sat in his Jeep longer than he normally did, smoking a second cigarette as he watched a gentle rain fall outside the fogged-up windows of his Jeep.

He thought about other routes that might take him home. He thought about his kids for some reason. He thought how he was just being stupid and getting himself all worked up over nothing.

There was no choice but to run the gauntlet.

When the sign cautioning the impending stop ahead flickered in the headlight's gleam, Trevor slowed. The headstones of the little country cemetery appeared somehow more sinister in the gloom of a late summer Midwestern drizzle, the distant flickers of occasional far-off lightning flashing off the wet stone.

Red tails lights glowed menacingly in the dampness.

The radio buzzed and began playing music, where just a few seconds before there had been only static.

Trevor flinched instinctively at the first note.

He was relieved to hear that it was a Carole King song. A song that he used to sing with his mother when Trevor was just a boy, sitting on his momma's lap in their back garden.

A nostalgically pleasant and heavy sigh left his body.

After checking for cross-traffic, Trevor started accelerating through the four-way stop. With the cemetery safely in the rearview mirror, and the radio playing cooperatively, he even relaxed enough to begin singing along to the song, just as he had done as a little boy.

Images of his mother flickered inside his head.

Trevor thought he could smell her perfume, that oddly comforting fragrance so familiar to him since he was little.

The sight of the disabled semi-truck, jackknifed across both lanes of a rain-soaked curve of State Route 36 abruptly cut off the sound of Trevor's voice singing:

"It's too late, baby, now. It's..."

He didn't apply the brakes.

No scream rang out.

While Trevor's mind frantically processed the impending eternity of his final breath, the radio in the Jeep switched back to simply playing static.

Martinsburg Daily Herald
Friday August 4, 2000

SEMI COLLISION KILLS ONE

Local Martinsburg resident, Trevor Bedford, 34, was killed overnight when his vehicle collided with a disabled semi-truck on Indiana State Route 36, south of Woltonville. The driver of the semi sustained minor injuries and declined hospitalization. The accident remains under investigation.

Plot E

I

Lester Bower's peg never quite fit properly in someone else's hole. But over the years he had learned to force it in anyway. Through the thin veneer of disingenuous charms and his penchant for dropping fast-talk promises in a small Midwestern Martinsburg, Indiana backwater starving for that temporary attention, Lester earned a dishonest living while the rest of the country was distracted patriotically fighting the first years of the war.

Born in Woltonville, Indiana in the hot summer of 1923, Lester Bower was not blessed with many positive influences. His father, Edward, a drinker by choice and a jackoff by all trades, often failed to make it home to the failing family farm barely clinging to existence on the outskirts of town, choosing instead to drink and sleep his way through the farm community currents of a surprisingly receptive Woltonville population.

Lester's mother, Beatrice, contributed very little towards helping him prepare for a responsible Hoosier adulthood. Having learned early, barely fifteen and already married and socially tethered to a drunkenly unpredictable and chronically flaccid Edward, that she had no one upon whom she might lean, Beatrice ultimately was forced to drop any pretext of decency and resigned herself to doing what must be done in order to feed her family.

Lester never really learned how to work the farm. At least not successfully. But was he still clever enough to have educated himself behind doors shamefully closed, originally using dusty, second-hand textbooks as a mental barrier to help drown out the sounds of his mother satisfying her nightly negotiations, those sweaty and grunt-filled transactions conducted behind that closed door in exchange for acquiring the monetary means of keeping the too many creditors at bay.

The Bower family, seeking the possibilities afforded by better opportunities elsewhere, eventually moved to the outskirts of Martinsburg, Indiana right before the stock market came crashing down. It was the worst possible time for such a turbulent change in the established family dynamic. With the economy of the country spiraling ever lower, the Bower's held on as best they could with deeply ingrained Hoosier thriftiness. But it was seldom enough and far too many of Lester's childhood dinners consisted simply of sleep, because an earlier bedtime was the best meal the struggling family could afford.

During the drab fall of 1938, with the economy slipping and the threats of another war billowing on the far-off horizons of Europe, life for the Bowers was grim amidst the backdrop of a struggling nation's great depression.

Edward began drinking more and more. And stumbling home less and less. Beatrice retaliated against the daily abandonment by intentionally paying more debts, even the ones that were in no real danger of rolling overdue. Lester continued unsupervised, learning the many scams and rackets of a Martinsburg underbelly thriving in the blackness of the shadows cast by more patriotically rationed markets, once America had officially joined the war.

On a frost-covered October morning, Edward stumbled home shortly before a red sunrise lit itself above a still sleeping Indiana city. Half-tripping through the bedroom door, Edward was enraged to find his wife in the arms of a naked man, one visibly more successful...and better endowed.

Three shots- the first two in quick succession, the final one moments after, startled Lester from a dreamless sleep. Confused initially at the sounds, he pulled himself from underneath a thin quilt that was more patches than it was actual blanket, and went to investigate.

Seeing his parents dead had a strange impact on Lester. He felt a resonating emptiness. They had never really committed to parenting him, leaving Lester to find his own way in life. He almost felt relief from knowing that he was no longer entangled in that doomed household, so tragically flawed.

A young, and some would say handsome, Lester gravitated back to the familiar streets of Martinsburg, once the bank foreclosed on the family house. He relied upon his charms and elaborate scams to dishonestly obtain his daily sustenance. And sometimes, he convincingly employed his natural capacity for breaking hearts, just to help him find some company, no matter how brief.

Lester slept in unlocked garages and in alleys and under porches. He begged and he stole and he scammed. He fucked and smoked and drank his way into any number of compromising situations, always on the hustle for the next easy buck. Or the next willing partner, so easily manipulated for his personal amusement.

Lester got himself involved with a local judge's young daughter and that fleshy entanglement resulted in real, birthable trouble. He had used his crafty words and seductive charms to get under her dress that chilly night in the back of the cemetery behind the local church. A night where rough, dirty fingers probed relentlessly for a softer weakness.   A   night   where   sweet,   but   insincere, endearments   were   offered   until   at   last   reservations crumbled in the face of a fervently targeted onslaught.

That heated and intimate indiscretion ultimately led to the kind of trouble that ruins the reputation of an unwed young girl living in the constriction of Indiana small town values-backed judgement and scorn. The kind of trouble that left few avenues of escape available to a slippery 21-year-old, near penniless drifter, scamming his way through sections of society in which he had no real business meddling. The kind of trouble that made it easier for the disapprovingly judgmental judge to offer Lester a simple choice- join the army, or go to jail.

A cursory medical exam, some forms signed, a quick oath unenthusiastically uttered and Lester Bower was duly enlisted into an army desperate for fresh bodies to feed the meatgrinder of a two-theatre conflict spanning most of the globe.

As the crowded and rowdy train filled with uninducted soldiers started chugging towards the reporting center noted on his neatly typed orders, Lester Bower smirked to himself. Outside his train window he watched his problems, and all of Martinsburg, slip away behind him.

II

Training.

And then even more training endured before Lester Bower was shipped off to the European Theatre of Operations to join the 41st Reconnaissance Squadron of 11th Armor Division, 3rd US Army.

The Battle of the Bulge was a recent memory by the time Lester took his place in the field. Hitler's mighty Reich was in the death throes of its final days, leaving Lester with almost no meaningful combat experience. Even when those opportunities for possible action arose- at haphazard crossroads intersecting random Austrian villages, or in nameless fields of nameless farms, Lester always managed to somehow find a reason to avoid danger.

Saturday May 5th, 1945 was a typical spring day on the continent. The morning was born grey and it drizzled briefly in the cool early hours before eventually giving way to hesitant sunshine. The air remained damp enough that sounds seemed somehow muffled, and that acoustic anomaly caused the recon patrol, ordered to move out in force, to be even more alert.

The soldiers smelled it before they saw it.

They smelled it over their own body odors and stale cigarette smoke polluting the funky atmosphere within their half-tracks. They smelled it over the exhaust fumes of the engines running hot and hard on the road to liberation.

The sights that married themselves to the pungent odor of death on an almost incomprehensible scale caused the soldiers of the 41st Reconnaissance Squadron to pause. Some even vomited.

The sharp bark of an officer's order snapped them back into action and the efforts to bring some relief and semblance of order to the abused inmates of a freshly liberated Mauthausen concentration camp started almost immediately.

Runners ran and couriers carried, while radios chattered in camouflaged vehicles, sending out the news of their gruesome discovery, asking desperately for any assistance available in the surrounding area to come immediately to their aid.

Half-empty canteens and canned rations were shared freely. Encouraging words were expressed. Meager stocks of medicine were distributed to those most likely to survive.

Amidst all the confusion of the initial efforts at forming some sense of organization, Lester caught sight of a young girl from the camp, standing in the door of a strange building, shielding her eyes instinctively against the unpredictable rays of sunshine.

She was dirty and unbelievably thin; there was barely enough substance to her frame to even cast a shadow in the doorway behind her. But she was still alive amidst incalculable death, leaning against the first doorway of the sonderbauten, the "special room."

Lester was attracted instantly to her vulnerability. And the way her stained and striped prison dress hung limply against her body, projecting a helplessness that just could not be ignored, enticed him. While his squad mates scrambled around, trying to accomplish something meaningful amongst the incomprehensible tragedy surrounding them, Lester focused on an entirely different kind of liberation.

He walked directly towards her, offering her in his extended hand both a Hershey Bar and pack of Luckys. These generous gifts were backed by the same coy look Lester had often employed successfully on women back in his Martinsburg days.

Lester expertly manipulated the situation and they disappeared into the shadows of the building together.

The sound of a dress tearing barely registered amongst the surrounding collective suffering. Lester violated her, roughly, and repeatedly, in the same room where she had been used nearly every night since her train had been uncharacteristically redirected from the unique horrors of the original destination of Auschwitz.

That first day of reckoning at Munchausen dictated that Agnieszka was young enough, and malleable enough, to join the pale and bruised woman of the camp brothel. There, every night since her fateful selection, between the hours of 8 and 10 p.m.- and through most of Sunday afternoons- Agnieszka had no choice but to spread herself out, the schedule of her femininity and sex rigidly dictated in 15-minute sessions by the Germans guards for the benefit of those the captors deemed deserving of receiving such a rare reward.

Agnieszka stopped struggling; her flesh was growing cool. Lester was so consumed by his devious fixations that he failed to realize that he was being watched through the slightly open door by a member of his squad, sent with very specific orders to find out "where the fuck that new guy from Indiana is because he sure as fuck ain't here."

Lester Bower was quickly led away by the angered and disgusted members of his squad, their .45s and rifles and bayonets all pointed at his back and head, directing the way towards his incarceration.

Agnieszka's body, still partially nude and slumped over a stained and splintering table, was diligently inspected and documented by superior ranking officers. Once the evidence had been collected, her body was added to the pile of greater death outside, the stacks of human corpses in various stages of decomposition, that had been waiting their turn in a disposal process devoid of any compassionate dignity. The discarded remnants of an unforgiving humanity gone mad bore silent witness as Agnieszka joined their stack.

III

Lester Bower was unanimously found guilty at his general court martial, argued at Divisional HQ and was sentenced to death by hanging. By regulation, every death sentence is automatically appealed under the Code of Military Justice, so Lester was transferred to HMP Shepton Mallet back in England where he awaited his fate.

The upper court found no reason to question the verdict and upheld the original sentence. President Truman, under the auspices of the Articles of War, signed the paperwork necessary to execute a citizen soldier.

The summer evening in August 1947 when Lester was led to that flat-roofed red brick building holding the gallows' secrets, its color standing out against the dullness of the surrounding stone prison structures, was cool and cloudy.

Inside the execution block adjoining one of the prison wings, the moon refused to shine through the single window, though the hour was approaching 1 a.m.

Heavy footsteps scuffed and echoed in the narrow building, all the way up to the gallows kiss.

A voice, gruff and official, read the charges and final verdict, cruelly and intentionally stretching out the last moments of a condemned man standing at the edge of his eternity.

With the charges dutifully read, Lester was asked if he wanted to make a final statement.

He answered them only with his silence.

Panicked breath, hot and claustrophobic, vibrated inside the darkness of the hood slipped over Lester's head from behind.

Before the lever was shifted, pulling the world out from underneath him, a frantic deal was made with the Devil because in that moment, Lester knew for certain that God was just not listening.

A feeling of being momentarily weightless the split-second after the trap door underneath bound feet opened surged through Lester's remaining senses.

He instinctively drew in a final breath and subconsciously flexed against the bindings holding tight.

Gravity inevitably took hold of a body's weight, pulling down briskly enough that Lester did not even have time to comprehend the sound of a guilty neck snapping.

POSTSCRIPT

The mortal remains of Lester Bower were removed from the gallows with little fanfare or ceremony. Disinterested soldiers cut his body free and wrapped it rather haphazardly inside a plain cotton mattress cover- the dishonorable dead of the victorious Allied Expeditionary Force did not warrant the consideration of even a simple casket.

The body, enshrouded in its nontraditional wrappings, was originally interred in Section X of Brookwood Cemetery, back beside the garden shed holding the tools of the cemetery grounds crew. In 1949, however, the body of Lester and his surrounding companions in crime were unceremoniously disinterred and moved to the waiting confines of the Oise-Aisne cemetery in France, just to the northwest of Paris.

Plot E of that cemetery is unique in that its location is not listed on any official map. It is situated across a road, purposefully facing away from other, more honorable, burial plots. No flags ever fly over that unconsecrated ground, marked in rows of nameless markers. Mourners are actively discouraged from visiting.

A singular, undecorated grave in northern France, holding the body Lester Edward Bowers, bears a two-digit number carved into a plain rectangular stone of unimpressive size. The similar markers surrounding Lester's final resting place combine to form a palpably malevolent reminder of a "Greatest Generation's" hidden disgrace.

It is a small, unremarkable plot of unhallowed ground, a lasting dishonored testimony to the crisp fallibility of the underlying humanity belonging to men and boys destined to never grow old. Ninety-four disappointing sons that no one ever mourns, or remembers. Ninety-four flawed soldiers who embarrassed their nation and betrayed civility. Ninety-four souls who will never rest in peace under foreign soil, a long way from home.

Lest we forget...

Rock-A-Bye-Baby

I

"Sir, we have to ask you to leave now. You're scaring some of the other customers," said a hesitant voice, interrupting Patrick's phone call.

It was not the first time a disheveled Patrick Wagner was asked to vacate a store. Sometimes, he was asked politely. Other times, a random employee confronted the agitated homeless customer causing a raucous inside their store. And they always managed to somehow dehumanize Patrick by the way he was asked to leave.

Occasionally, either store security, or a member of the Martinsburg Police Department were called to the scene to assist in Patrick's removal. It was usually the result of unmedicated moments spinning him towards another terrorizing episode manically spilling out inside another thrift store.

Ten years previously, early in his fourteenth year, Patrick Wagner had been diagnosed with bipolar disorder. That disability punched into his life after a particularly heated incident at Martinsburg Central High that culminated in a lengthy suspension for the ragingly adolescent Patrick.

The unfamiliar surroundings of a new school, coupled with the abusive nature of his bullying classmates, sparked Patrick into an unexpected rage during a shop class. It resulted in stitches, the threat of numerous lawsuits, and an innocent classmate who could now only count to nine and a half.

Patrick was not allowed to return to school until he had been evaluated by a medical professional. Martinsburg Central High, wanting to ensure the safety of students and staff, and to protect the district from any sort of legal action, insisted.

The cultural stigmas associated with the scourge of mental illness held by a tightly knit, God-fearing Hoosier heartland were just beginning to recede during the late 1990s. Awareness and tolerance were both growing into a grudgingly pressured acceptance, the hushed embarrassments transformed within the hesitant embrace of new treatments.

Simply putting a name on Patrick's inconsistent behaviors helped his mother, Stephanie. The diagnosis offered some solace to a struggling single mother trying her best to provide meaningful care for a child she just simply did not understand. And, if she was bluntly honest with herself- something Stephanie rarely allowed- a child that she struggled to love.

Stephanie Wagner was born in the upper end of the 1960s, an unwanted by-product of the Summer of Love. Her mother, Barbara, had naively hopped into the waiting promises of a VW wagon heading for the west coast, driven by a patchouli-scented wanna-be poet. And she followed those promises, and that man, all the way to San Francisco.

But the optimistically exuberant so-called "summer of love" soon twisted into a bastardized caricature of itself in the heated shame of a sexually dysfunctional, and mentally abusive, transcontinental relationship. A visibly pregnant, and venereally infected, Barbara hitchhiked alone all the way back to the judgmental confines of Martinsburg. And once home, she had to suffer the critical scowls and biblically backed dispersions cast by her religiously inflexible family.

Stephanie spent the entirety of her formative years trying her best to live up to the lofty ideals and paisley-fringed aspirations from that summer of her birth. She looked for love whenever, and from whomever, she could find it.

And the hormone-fueled, temporary coupling she found in the back of Aaron Tibby's carpeted panel van on a mild summer night in 1981 resulted in an unwanted pregnancy of her own, her teenage uterus mirroring the same reproductive carelessness that her mother's had gestated.

Patrick Wagner was born on a wet and humid Indiana August morning in the unnamed summer of 1982. His birth was free of both complication and impediment and his young mother was excited to have someone in her life who would love her without question or complaint.

That joy that Stephanie felt would quickly recede in the crushing responsibility of parenting, as a screaming, crying, and shitting obstruction grew older, complicating the fulfillment of her many desires.

Patrick was not an intentionally difficult child; he just did not know any better. The constant revolving door of short-term male influences in his life offered little stability. The undiagnosed issues bubbling under the surface of Patrick's developing personality had yet to fully surface. The many nights spent alone as he grew older instilled Patrick with a growing sense of both abandonment and paranoia. His mother stayed out later and later, shaking her ass to earn dirty fistfuls of cash when not gunning rails of coke in the seedy back-room VIP sections of the club.

Stephanie died in one of the sticky back rooms of the club, the private dens of debauchery set up by the management of Show N' Tails to provide a place for the girls to earn the club an extra source of illicit income. There they were free from the prying eyes of local law enforcement and the many governmental agencies involved in state licensing matters. At one point, Show N' Tails was the best cum-stained secret in all of Martinsburg and Stephanie thrived there.

That Thursday night, towards the end of another glitter-highlighted shift on a stage crowded with crumpled, desperate dollar bills, Stephanie led one of her more regular customers into the back of the club. She was hungry more for his cash and stash of drugs, than for the moderate bulge curving out the front of his well-worn blue jeans.

The grinding dance shared in a hollow room echoed back grunts of bad decisions, both bareback and dispassionate. Beneath sweaty bodies, a stained couch creaked in sync to the shitty club music pumping in through crackling speakers.

The drugs they shared after the gyrations ceased were meant to be a celebratory treat to two lost and broken people who managed to find one another amongst the lower echelons of Martinsburg society.

A nameless familiar stranger used his rig and took the first taste. Stephanie followed suit, eager to feel the comforting numbness flowing through insatiable veins.

There was a fatal miscalculation in the rush to get high and the shot that Stephanie injected was a hot one. She slumped and foamed into an unconsciousness from which she would never awake. A nameless man slunk out the door, leaving behind just another used-up junkie slut.

The first indication Patrick had that something serious had happened was when the Martinsburg police cruiser rolled up in front of the house shortly before dawn.

He had been awake all night. But not out of worry for his mother- Patrick had discouragingly grown accustomed to her coming home late. Or sometimes, not at all.   He was instead struggling through the insomniatic mania of another episode unfolding inside his unpredictable mind.

But even in an agitated, raving state, Patrick could clearly connect the dots and he just knew when the officers stepped out of the cruiser to make the notification that his mother was not coming home.

Ever.

Stopping only long enough to grab his leather jacket and the little bit of money he had managed to hide from Stephanie's desperate and addiction-driven hands, Patrick raced out the back door and disappeared into the first light of a new Martinsburg day.

III

Patrick tried his best to remain undetected, relying upon his wits to survive. The cajoling voices occasionally heard inside his head urged him to refrain from trusting anyone, least of all any sort of authority figure. For the rest of that summer, and most of an Indiana autumn, Patrick managed to remain just another lonely homeless figure, lurking in the shadows.

The threat of a first winter alone, blowing in hard and unexpectedly early, demanded a revision of Patrick's original plan; the unpredictability of the Indiana weather pushed him to seek out some sort of assistance. Though eventually saved from living raw out in the elements, Patrick merely exchanged one danger for another as he was thrown into the crushing grind of an abuse-filled Child Protective Services.

The turnstile of revolving foster care families, all seemingly out for personal gain, provided the worst possible environments for an unpredictable teenager. Medication was provided only in intermittent surges, usually timed around the predetermined visits of disinterested and overworked case workers. Love was just another commodity withheld, though illicit attempts were made to get physical with Patrick on numerous occasions.

Patrick gained his freedom the day he turned 18, legally aging him out of an indifferent system punting him back out onto the streets.

"Sir, we are going to have to ask you to leave now. Some of the other customers are complaining that you're scaring them."

The stare Patrick gave the nervous Salvation Army cashier while still holding a phone receiver up to his ear caused her to back away from him. He continued that stare until she had vacated the haphazardly stocked office supply aisle entirely.

Only then did he return to a conversation that had been threatening to grow heated before the inconsiderate interruption.

Patrick knew from experience shopping at second-hand thrift stores that they seldom sported any sort of in-store security, relying instead upon a hastily dialed 911 call if things spiraled out of control. And he knew that if he did not overtly threaten anyone, and did not cause any damage to either store or inventory, in most cases, they'd refrain from making that call.

Over the years spent living under bridges, in back alleys, and if the weather turned cold, inside the heated stairways of any number of parking garages downtown, Patrick had taken quite a liking to shopping in stores that affordably marketed the cast-off flotsam of society. It was almost a voyeuristic experience for him and he enjoyed the little peeks into the lives of strangers living better lives.

Electronics especially appealed to him. And Patrick was often surprised at how many of the radios still worked. At least for him. He enjoyed turning on the random old stereos and handheld radios sitting unplugged on the shelf, and listening to the music that only he could hear.

It was a Saturday afternoon trip to the closest Salvation Army store, the one serving as an economic boundary just on the south side of downtown Martinsburg, that Patrick randomly picked up a phone receiver. It opened a whole new world.

He did not expect to hear a voice answer him when he offered a jokingly insincere "Hello?" when he put the cold black handset up to his ear that first time.

In the bipolarity of his mind, Patrick created conversations nearly every time he picked up an abandoned thrift store telephone. Usually, the unfamiliar voices proclaimed to be those of some unknown relative from the family that had abandoned him.

The conversations spanned the gamut of human peculiarities, depending on the swing of his emotions and the diligence of his meager attempts at street-level self-medicating. But that delusional connection allowed Patrick an opportunity to channel his mania through cast-off electronics in a relatively harmless fashion.

After making his telephonic discovery, Patrick realized that the older the phone was, the older the relative speaking to him. Their conversations stretched back through several imagined generations, each one speaking to Patrick with targeted intent.

Sometimes, those conversations nudged him into making good decisions, like sleeping a night in the shelter if the weather was going to be bad. Other times, Patrick was goaded into questionable actions, usually revolving around some spike in his drug consumption.

The furtive voices whispered for Patrick to go ahead and indulge in the many secretive urges coursing through a manic body. They teased and taunted a drive simmering just beneath the surface.

When not pushing a more sinister agenda, those imaginary voices of long dead relatives championed the cause of evil in hushed suggestions of opportunity. Like the day Patrick was nearly caught pickpocketing that elderly woman for no other reason than she had left her purse unattended. That inattention led to a temptation impossible to ignore and when the voice crackling and wheezing on the other end of a disconnected phone line gave the all clear, Patrick lifted the wallet out of her handbag.

The voice on the phone Patrick picked up that Saturday afternoon in the back of the Salvation Army was one he was not expecting to hear. Unlike all the others, the ones constantly urging him deeper into the turbulent waters of a moral ambiguity, the one he heard that day was familiar and that attachment helped fuel the fire of Patrick's gaze staring down the hapless cashier.

Because it was his mother's voice on the phone.

"But Mom, I just don't understand. How could you do that to me? How could you just leave me like that?" Patrick asked into the phone when the cashier had been shooed away. "Didn't you love me?"

"Of course I did, baby. I just didn't love myself very much back then and you got caught up in that. And I'm so very sorry."

"I don't understand, Momma. I know that I wasn't what you wanted. But I did try. I really did. I just wanted you to be proud of me," Patrick sobbed, the sound of his tears beginning to attract unwanted attention from a few hapless shoppers.

"I am proud of you, Monkey," the voice on the phone replied, using a nickname Patrick hadn't heard in many years. It caused even more tears to flow down cheeks now streaked wet through the grit and grime of too many months spent living on the streets. "But now I need you to do something for me."

"Anything, momma," Patrick replied, weakly.

"It's time for you to come home now, baby. I know how hard it's been for you and you did a good job. You really did. And I'm proud of you. But, you need to come home."

"Okay, momma."

Patrick grabbed the phone off the shelf and walked to the back of the store where the changing rooms were located. Every room was empty, but still he selected the one designated for the handicapped as it afforded a bit more room.

He closed the door behind him, turning the lock on the doorknob to guarantee privacy.

Ignoring the wood bench attached to the wall, Patrick sat on the cold floor. His back leaned against the now locked door. Across from him, a reflection stared. Patrick took in the details bouncing back at him. The stained clothes. The defeated look of exhausted surrender. Fingers, grimy and calloused from digging out a living on the inhospitable streets of an indifferent Martinsburg. The lines the hot tears made on his scruffy, unwashed face.

Once settled on the floor, Patrick returned the phone receiver to his ear.

"Momma? Are you still there?" he asked meekly.

"Yes, baby. I'm still here."

Muffled sobs echoed in the confines of the changing room.

"Don't cry, Monkey. It's all going to be okay," the disconnected voice offered, soothingly.

Patrick drew in a deep breath and exhaled. He thought about his mother's comforting touch. He wondered if he should get high. Or at least smoke a cigarette. But the voice on the phone didn't give him that chance.

"It's time, baby. Come home to your momma."

"Will it hurt?" Patrick asked meekly.

"No. I promise. Now, do as your momma says. It's been too long since we've been together."

"Okay, momma," Patrick replied.

He dropped the receiver from his ear long enough to untwist the tie holding the phone cord neatly together and unclipped the other end from the back of the phone.

Looking over his shoulder, Patrick reached up and twisted the cord several times around the doorknob of the changing room door. Making sure that there wasn't much slack in the line, he wrapped the remaining cord around his neck.

Putting the phone back up to his ear, Patrick asked, "Is that okay?"

"That's perfect, baby. Now just slide down a little bit and it will all be over before you know it."

"But, momma? I'm scared," came Patrick's feeble reply.

"Oh, Monkey. There's no reason to be scared. I'll be right here."

"You promise?" Patrick asked, hopefully.

"Yes, baby. I promise. I'll be right here. And, I will even sing to you, just like I used to when you were little, if you think that will help."

"Yes, please," was Patrick's meek reply. "Momma?"

"Yes, baby?"

"I love you."

"I love you, too. Now just slide down. It'll be just like going to sleep. And your momma is right here to tuck you in."

"Okay, momma."

Patrick allowed his body to limply slide down. The cord, twisted around his neck, held.

He heard his mother's voice starting to sing.
 "Rock-a-bye baby, in the tree top. When the wind blows, the cradle will rock. When the bough breaks, the cradle will fall and down will come baby, cradle and all..."

Room 302

I

"Are you kidding me? I just paid that!"

Jennifer's voice was raw and raspy from working the breakfast shift at a greasy diner, crowded with even greasier customers. She had adjusted her hours that day to allow time for a stop at the store after work before picking up her son, Jacob, from his daytime care takers. Struggling through that morning, fueled by caffeine and cigarettes chain-smoked during her breaks, made her sound, and feel, rough.

They needed groceries and Jennifer had rationed out the coupons enough to fill her cart, ensuring that the cupboards would be moderately stocked. At least for the foreseeable future.

Jennifer mentally juggled her finances at the store before committing to the swipe of an unpredictable card and was audibly relieved when APPROVED blinked on the screen. That feeling of relief was temporary, however. An overdue electric bill, marked with an accusatory DISCONNECTION NOTICE, had been tucked into the screen of her door, waiting to welcome her home.

It was going to be another pinched month in the Howell household. But then, it had always been tight.

Jennifer Howell was born into a clear fall Martinsburg day in November of 1972. She was immediately welcomed into the loving clutches of her deeply Catholic Hoosier family, elated at the joyous new addition. A precocious child, Jennifer often struggled to spread her wings within the judgmental confines of her extended congregation's constant gaze.

Despite the limitations and curfews imposed religiously upon her, Jennifer managed to keep up socially with her much faster friends. She owned an acid washed jean jacket with graffiti and frayed cuffs, a crumbled half-pack of contraband Marlboro Lights and pink disposable lighter stuffed into a pocket. She knew, and loved, all the big rock songs from all the big hair bands, rocking their way through the rural Indiana haze of the early 1980s. She explored her body, shunning the born-in guilt to finger out the bubbling urges of her tingling flesh. Jennifer indulged those yearnings first because her body was the one thing over which she could exert some sense of control, but then later enjoyed simply for feeling that sinfully hot flush.

Her stubborn defiance, coupled with an escalating sexuality, contributed to Jennifer choosing her legs as a validation-seeking replacement for the unseen wings of faith. They were the only gospel she could spread and Jennifer excelled at it. Initially her indiscretions remained undetected during her weekly Catholic interrogation session. But it was just more lies inside of another dark closet.

Her reckless, approval-seeking behaviors caught up with Jennifer. Even in the medieval shadows of the neighborhood confessional, there was no possibility of hiding a belly literally bulging with sin.

II

It was a humid Saturday night fall cornfield party when Nathan Whigman drank Jennifer into parting her legs on that itchy wool blanket hidden in the rows of Indiana corn, just in earshot of their friends still drinking and passing the bowl at an impromptu barn party.

There was little that Jennifer remembered from the night Jacob was conceived. Just the smell of the hot corn and just how disappointedly small Nathan's member felt when compared to all his previous bragging. That should have been the first indicator that he wasn't really man enough for Jennifer, a suspicion later proven when Nathan immediately dropped out of the picture soon after Jennifer confessed the conception.

In a misguided attempt to spare her family the communal shame of her fertility, Jennifer left Central High before her indiscretion began to show. Through the entirety of her pregnancy, Jennifer was fed nourishing homemade food for the health of the developing fetus, all served with a complimentary side order of judgmental guilt, just for religious zest.

Jacob's birth was a difficult one. Various complications extended Jennifer's labor for the better part of that spring Indiana day and when that last push contracted, little Jacob Evan Howell was introduced into the world.

Jennifer's parents told her that Jacob was her penance for her sinful ways. Had she not strayed from the virtuous path, she would not have been burdened with a child who was beginning to display every indication of having diminished mental capacities.

Despite his unimmaculate conception, Jennifer's family pressured her to keep Jacob. They did not want their genetic embarrassment adopted out, only to eventually be traced back to their family honor. It was better to keep their invalid secret closer to home.

Had her parents not been blindsided by that drunk driver on Statesville Road shortly after Jennifer and Jacob had moved in with them, perhaps they would have been around to help Jennifer navigate the crush of single motherhood. But in the blink of a car's fatal crumpling, Jennifer lost the entirety of her safety net.

Her parent's estate was settled swiftly. Even Jennifer's younger brother, who had handled the estate, felt bad calling her with the sobering news that their parents had left the bulk of their assets to the Church. Neither Jennifer, nor Jacob, were provided for in their final wishes.

III

It was a struggle.

Even during the earliest days, when Jennifer could look down at a squirming, giggling little boy and pretend that he was "normal," things were rough.

The money from the State only covered Jacob's special needs child care. Everything else was a stretch. Jennifer dutifully danced that monthly routine of the working poor, struggling to keep their heads above disconnections.

Jennifer always worked at the best jobs willing to accept her meager academic accomplishments and the scheduling demands of trying to single handedly raise a developmentally challenged child.

It was mostly low paying waitressing gigs that Jennifer landed, literally putting her ass on the line daily for the sake of maybe a bigger tip. The jobs were always easy to find, but difficult for Jennifer to hold as her responsibilities grew in tandem with Jacob's physical development.

As he grew older and stronger, it became more of a challenge to keep his hormonal shifts in balance, both at home in the evenings and during his daily development. After the masturbation incident, Jennifer was advised to authorize Jacob for a course of maintenance medication to ease his hormonal urges to a more realistically manageable level.

She intentionally put off that decision for as long as possible, knowing what the care takers meant behind their euphemistic words and cheaply printed pamphlets. Desperate to hold on to the little bit of help she had for Jacob's care, Jennifer grudgingly signed the paperwork necessary to keep him enrolled in the program.

She was in line at the pharmacy, picking up that initial prescription for Jacob, when Jennifer collapsed.

Jennifer had been feeling run down and drained for months, but simply attributed those feelings to the grind of her schedule and the fact, confirmed every morning when looking into the bathroom mirror, that she was getting undeniably older.

At first, the barely affordable walk-in clinic diagnosed her with an unspecified infection and prescribed her antibiotics, advising her to follow up with her regular physician. The antibiotics seemed to make no difference and when it got to the point that she could barely get herself out of bed in the morning, Jennifer knew that something was seriously wrong.

A brutally efficient series of painful tests administered shortly after walking into the Emergency Room of Martinsburg General Hospital confirmed Jennifer's suspicions.

The diagnosis of leukemia shortly after the turn of the 21st Century was not necessarily the death sentence it had been in preceding years. There was hope in the transplanting of marrow which, while still somewhat in its medical infancy, had already shown great promise.

Terrified at her diagnosis, Jennifer surrendered herself to the care of Dr. Reinstein. There was a calming quality to his manner and Jennifer found herself grasping desperately at any straw Dr. Reinstein offered.

Because she had to take care of Jacob.

While perhaps a grey area of moral ambiguity given his diminished mental capacity, Jacob could be a viable marrow donor and possibly save his mother's life. If he saved her, then Jennifer could continue to be there for him. That was the justification she held close to her heart as the testing began, Jacob's cries and screams echoing down the fluorescent corridor of Martinsburg General Hospital.

IV

Jennifer's doctor could never prove it medically, but his experience told him that it was not the cancer that claimed Jennifer. In fact, they had located a compatible marrow donor the week she died. Everything had been pointing towards a more hopeful prognosis. But there was nothing in the whole of Dr. Reinstein's medical training that guided him in the treatment of a broken heart.

And Jennifer's heart did break that grey Indiana morning when informed, rather clinically, that it was a genetic impossibility that Jacob was her biological son. The lab results, run multiple times for confirmation, were the definitive proof.

Someone had committed an atrociously callous mistake by inexcusably switching two unrelated children. Children, unguarded and innocent, supposedly under the watchful care of the overworked maternity ward staff at Martinsburg General Hospital.

Jennifer spent her whole life taking care of a problem that was never supposed to have been hers. Her every hope and her every small-town Indiana dream had been sacrificed for the sake of fighting an unwinnable battle genetically belonging to some strangers.

Jacob would never be smart. He would never have the chance to mature like a "normal" boy. He would never be considered attractive. He would never be anything but a broken, and sometimes violent, burden.

But Jennifer tried her best to love him anyway.

As Jennifer spent her final hours suffering in Room 302, she wondered about her other child, that biological baby boy of whom she was robbed.

Was he kind? Was he handsome? Was he going to be successful? Was he intelligent? Would he even ever know about her?

As a warm spring Indiana rain drizzled outside a third floor Martinsburg General Hospital room window, staining the air lightly with the scent of lilacs growing outside, a machine screamed out a shrill warning in Room 302.

A blur of masked strangers rushed to struggle against the various alarms.

Sharp orders barked. Numbers, cold and clinical, yelled out. Heroic efforts made with gloved hands.

Three miles south, a block away from the limestone facade of the Martinsburg office of Child Protective Services, other gloved hands were also busy at work.

They were aggressively struggling to guide a combatively uncooperative seventeen-year-old body, surging with adolescent hormones and a deep fear of separation, into a plain white van.

Jacob looked fearfully out of the wire mesh covered window of the nondescript Child Protective Services transport vehicle, confused at an unfamiliar Martinsburg blur rushing past.

He did not understand where they were going.

Jacob just wondered if his mom was going to be there to meet him.

Martinsburg Daily Herald
Tuesday, July 23, 2002

Jennifer Howell, 30, lost her brave battle against cancer and was called home to Jesus on Friday. She is survived by her son, Jacob, 13, and brother, Andrew, 27. No services or calling announced. Internment at Pleasant Hills Cemetery.

A Smile in the Sunshine

"Pulse rate is slowing. Resps are getting shallow. It won't be long now."

"It won't be long now," she said, her chestnut hair dancing back in the slipstream of the wind hugging the contours of the little convertible. "And I know the perfect place, too. Just wait until you see it!" As if to punctuate her excitement, she stomped on the accelerator and the little car zipped down the country road.

He smiled, just as he always did whenever she was near. He had nothing to fear and nothing to worry about when in her charge, so he looked out at the scenery flying past in great blurs of a country medley. Fragments of scenes became more focused and the way they seemed suspended against the backdrop of rushing time made perfect sense. There was a small black cat hunting her prey. A red barn, battered by the weather of a hundred seasons stood sentinel on a gentle rise of Indiana farmland, watching patiently over a playground of birds and small creatures, all out enjoying the early spring weather. Winter had finally released her grip upon the land and all creatures, himself included, were out basking themselves in the glory of a Midwestern spring afternoon.

"I'm sorry to say that his condition will only worsen at this point. All we can do now is to make him comfortable."

"Hey you, 'Mister Star Gazer,' you still with me over there?" she asked, her voice penetrating his thoughts like a flashlight through the smoke of his favorite cigarettes. "If you aren't comfortable, I can always stop for a bit, though we really don't have too much farther to go."

Her eyes left the road and caught his. He should have been unnerved that she wasn't really driving anymore, having abandoned her task at the wheel to better attend him. But the little car seemed to be doing just fine, purring along as if still benefiting from the guidance of her hands. He was not the least bit alarmed.

"Me? Oh, I am doing just fine. I can't imagine any other place that I would rather be right now."

"Are you sure?" she asked. "I'm not very convinced of your sincerity, mister." Her playful tone confused him.

"What do you mean?"

Again, she smiled, radiating warmth. She pointed behind him and asked, teasingly, "Then how do you explain that?"

He followed her outstretched finger with his eyes and when he had turned around, his mother's kitchen was there. He could still feel the vibration of the car beneath him; her presence never for a moment left him. But there was no doubt about it. He was in his childhood home.

Through the sepia light streaking in through the airy lace curtains he saw his mother, proudly wearing that silly apron he had given to her when he was seven. She was hard at work preparing a large meal and the steam flooding up from the pots and pans on the stove danced deliciously.

He could tell that she had a cake in the oven, the final stage of preparing his favorite meal—a true labor of love.

Looking up from her work his mother saw him for the first time. Smiling that wonderful smile of hers, full of love from the whole of the family history, she grabbed up her wooden spoon and gently scolded him.

"What took you so long? Didn't you know that you'd be late for dinner? Now run along and wash your hands. When you get back, I'll let you help me frost the cake."

"Momma?" he asked softly.

"What is it, child?" she asked, absently wiping the sweat from her brow.

In a weak voice, crowded with years of built-up emotion, the only words that he could manage were "I love you."

"Well, I love you, too. Now go do as I say. Dinner will be on before too long and I expect you to be here. Lord knows you kept me waiting long enough."

Just as quickly as it came upon him it was all gone. He looked over to her, feeling like a scared little boy, afraid of everything and understanding nothing. Maybe she would have some answers for him.

"It's okay, baby. It's always like that. In fact, I was surprised that it took as long as it did."

Great sobs racked his body; tears stained his cheeks. He could feel the car slow a little beneath him, but he didn't care. He wanted to be back with his Momma.

"I know how hard it is, really I do," she offered in consolation. Reaching out, she began running her fingers along the back of his neck, stroking him affectionately.

"It's like this for everybody. Well, for most people, anyway. We have time if you need me to stop for a break."

A great sigh left his body, releasing at once all the pent-up emotions boiling inside him. "No, I think I'll be okay. I just wish it didn't hurt so badly, that's all."

Alarmed, she quickly asked, "It hurts? Hurts in a good way, or hurts as in pain?"

"As in pain," he mumbled weakly.

"Oh, it shouldn't be like that at all. Let's see if we can do something about this."

Swerving off to the side of the road, she stomped on the brakes. The car came to a screeching stop in front of a telephone booth, the exact kind that he used to run any number of scams upon for free calls during his youth. He wondered what it was doing out here in the middle of what seemed to be nowhere, but the fire burning inside caused his mind to wander incoherently. The last clear thing he remembered was hearing her ask somebody to help. Because "it just shouldn't be like this at all."

"I think it is time to increase the dosage. Let's see how he responds to another 5 cc's."

When his senses returned to him, they were back out on the road. He was slumped down in his seat a bit and there was still some residual perspiration on his brow. But the gnawing pain inside his chest was gone.

"Feeling a bit better now?" she asked nervously, scanning his face for any telltale signs of discomfort.

"Yes, I am. What happened? Who did you call back there?"

She laughed out loud. "Oh, never mind about all that. You'll know soon and besides, I bet that before long you'll be the one out here driving."

"But I…" He had started to protest that he did not understand what was going on around him, but a glance from her was enough to cut him short. He had always trusted her, ever since their first date back when they were fifteen. And he saw no reason to begin questioning her now.

"Would you like to listen to the radio? It might help you to relax a bit. I know that you're full of questions, so maybe listening for a while will help put your mind at ease."

He half-shrugged in agreement and asked what she wanted to listen to as he reached down to turn on the radio.

"Oh, whatever's on," she replied, giving him a little wink.

Turning on the radio, he noticed for the first time that the radio in this car was the exact same model that he had installed into the first car he had ever owned. It was a painfully hot summer day when he put that radio in, swearing and cursing up a storm at his own incompetence. But he eventually succeeded and that radio lasted him for a great many years, finally being abandoned when the faceplate became cracked and he was forced to rely upon a paperclip to turn it on.

He turned his head up, looking at her, questioning her with his eyes. Still smiling, she gave him a nudge with her head, urging him to turn it on. Hesitantly, he pressed the ON button and was amazed by what he heard pushing out the speakers.

"Is that…?"

"Yes!" she giggled. "Isn't it wonderful? I was hoping that you'd be surprised!"

Across every channel of every radio band, he heard conversations. Conversations he already knew because they were ones he had already had. The lower he went with the channels, the younger his voice sounded and the higher he went, his voice became deeper and more grown up.

"Is that really me?" he asked incredulously.

"Yes, it is! Amazing, isn't it? Just think of the possibilities!"

He played and played with that radio, changing channels, and switching bands like a mad man. They were all there, even conversations with friends he had forgotten long ago. Some were too painful to listen to again so instead of reliving those, he quickly moved on, at complete liberty to change the channel to a happier time. Up and down the radio waves he went, listening to his life through the car speakers.

"If you want to hear something special, turn the channel down one station from where you are right now."

Intrigued, he did as he was instructed and changed the channel. It was her voice which greeted him and he had to smile despite himself. This was one conversation which he was never able to forget. Not ever.

"I remember that night," he said at last, looking over to her. "I have thought of it so many times that you probably wouldn't believe me if I were to tell you."

She turned and met his gaze of love with one of her own. "Oh, I'd believe it. I'd believe it because I already knew. That is part of the reason why I was chosen to drive you."

"But I don't..."

"Shhhh," she said, placing her delicate finger upon his lips to silence his question before he had a chance to ask. "You'll know in time. But it isn't my place to tell you. You will just have to trust me."

"You already know that I trust you."

She leaned in and gave him a kiss so sweet and so potent that it took his breath away. He could taste her life and her passions in that kiss, the glorious highs and the crushing disappointments. Everything that she was she shared with him and it left him stunned, struggling to breathe.

"His breathing is becoming agonal. Heart rate is going up and his pulse is coming down. I think that you'd better call in his family."

"He doesn't have any family, Doctor."

All at once her kiss was gone. She seemed frazzled and hectic. "We really must go now. We're going to be late."

"For what?" he asked.

But she did not answer him. She focused on her driving, the car hugging the road through the twists and turns. Everything rushed by him, but this time it was different. He gave thought to playing with the radio some more, but the idea offered little comfort. Instead, he returned to watching the scenery flashing before him. It surprised him how quickly the sun was setting.

"Do you see how quick the sun is going down over there? I wonder what it means."

"It means we are late."

"Late for what?"

With a sigh of completion, she reached down and turned the ignition to the OFF position. "To be here," she replied, and pointed back over his shoulder.

The farmland around him had melted away, no red barns or black cats or phone booths to be seen in any direction. He saw that the car was parked in a huge field of grain, swaying and bending in the great Midwestern twilight. They had parked at the base of a small hill behind which the sun was now rapidly descending.

"We'd better hurry. It would be bad for you to miss this."

She opened her door and stepped out of the car and motioned for him to do the same. When he stepped out into the field, he happened to notice that the car had left no tracks behind. Everything around him was perfect. The air was deliciously warm; the hum of innumerable insects married itself to the wind in a perfect harmony of nature. He would have been happy to stay in this one spot forever and he probably would have if she wasn't coaxing him on further.

"Come on! We have to hurry now!"

She stretched out her hand as he walked to the front of the car, taking his hand. Quickly they began the ascent up the small hill, though the movement was making it difficult for him to breathe. The pain was back inside his chest. But it felt different this time, though he was unable to fully explain the sensation.

"Can't we stop for a moment? I'm having trouble breathing. I need to rest."

"It's only a few more steps. I know you can make it."

With renewed determination he continued putting one foot in front of the other, following her up that little hill. What had seemed at first to be only a gentle slope was turning into the most difficult challenge of his life.

"V-Tach."

"Almost there," she said, gently pulling at his hand. "Trust me; I know you want to see this!"

The pain inside was building. His heart began beating strangely inside his chest. The smell of his mother's kitchen was in the air again.

"V-Fib. What should we charge to, Doctor?"

"Nothing. His chart says he's DNR."

"I'm coming," he said weakly.

"I know you are, baby. And you really aren't going to believe this!"

With a great sense of accomplishment, he took his final step onto the top of that little hill. All at once the universe opened up before him and he saw…

"Asystole," said the doctor, reaching up and turning off the EKG machine.

"Time of death, 16:47."

The Genesis of Fallibility

I

The Seed

"Yeah, babe. Everything is fine. You don't need to worry about him. We're just friends," Angelica said into her phone, hastily retrieved from her naked neighbor's nightstand. Cory admired the sag of her breasts when she stretched over him and he had to fight the urge to take the grab offered. He was mildly irritated that their heated afternoon had been inconveniently interrupted by the annoyance of a mediocre boyfriend calling to check in for the day. And Cory felt that entitled him to a compensatory grope.

Angelica's piercing blue gaze cut Cory off as she continued to straddle him during her conversation with another man. The penis that remained inside her was filling a need that the dick on the phone simply could not provide. Because that new penis had actually paid attention to its unfaithful surroundings, diligently taking note of how to provide meaningful pleasure by mixing just the right concoction of ownership, surrender, and thrust.

Cory readjusted the pillow under his head and tried his best to tune out her big voice in that small room reeking of their sexual explorations. He closed his grey eyes and focused his energies on trying to remain hard inside Angelica. It was a somewhat moist struggle. The emotional soundtrack of another relationship's death throes playing out right above Cory was not the most conducive environment in which to maintain full turgidity. But he tried his best to erect some semblance of durability.

Angelica met the intermittent, fleshy thrusts up from beneath her with some grinding tricks of her own. Coy looks were expressed. Nipples, foolishly pierced years ago to impress some unfulfilled crush, were pinched and twisted. Any sensation at her disposal was employed to help keep her current favorite dick hard inside her as she struggled to free herself from the previous one still jabbering in her ear.

"Okay, baby. We'll talk about it later tonight then," she said, attempting to end the conversation.

Angelica's hips rocked. The grinding pressure of her womanhood against his pelvis increased. She was getting close and Cory wondered what she was going to get off first, the phone, or herself.

"I know. This isn't easy for me, either, babe."

One of Angelica's hands held the phone, the other pressed into Cory's chest. Nails, manicured and unnecessarily expensive, dug into pectoral flesh.

"Is this really happening?" Cory thought to himself, both his mind and genitals curiously married together in a moment of perverted disbelief.

"Okay. I love you, too," the regret detectable in Angelica's voice was a tangible disconnect from the passions being expressed from her blushing flesh. Cory wasn't even sure she had hung up completely before letting her battered phone fall to the twin sized mattress.

He wondered if the call was disconnected.

But Angelica was too focused on the pleasure of her own arousal. Her other hand joined at Cory's chest, leaning forward, grinding for just the right angle. And it did not take her long.

Legs twitched. Fucked up words slipped through unclean lips. Nails dug deeper as a familiar flood of heated wetness rushed over Cory's exposed sex, immediately soaking the mattress with the dampness of their conjoined sin.

Cory should have realized then the instability of Angelica's unhealthy peculiarities. And just how deeply damaged she must have been in order to derive that much pleasure from sexualizing the awkward moment when two unstable relationships collide unexpectedly in the orbital pull of her sexual appetites.

Obviously, it was all about the attention. And the simmering desires. And the underlying brain-tingling delight of doing all the wrong things, with all the wrong people, at all the wrong times; she liked being naughty. It filled in for the other addictions she was no longer allowed to pursue quite as freely as she had in those days before she became a mother.

But Angelica Parker was a welcome distraction from the suffocating blandness of Cory Stiles' existence. She was chaos and she was sparking, uninhibited sexuality. She was an unrestrained temptation into which Cory had predictably tripped and, just like within the confines of those poorly worded cheesy sit-com jokes, he inevitably ended up with his dick buried inside her.

There wasn't much else happening on their relatively quiet block of West End Drive, down where

Pebble Creek, a durable tributary of Stone River, twists its way through the nicer parts of the blue-collared neighborhoods of Martinsburg. It felt good to be doing something- it felt even better to be doing someone.

Through the unification of their dishonest sex, both Angelica and Cory had found a heated, sweaty sanctuary from the crushing obligations of their suburban coexistence. It brought some color into the drabness of their expectations and it fucked new vigor into bedrooms hereto either ignored, or coldly unappreciated.

The mutual burden of their combined sins validated the weight of their needs. The chemistry of the uninhibited sessions excused their underlying immorality, at least in those uncontrolled reactions sucking and fucking explosively whenever they could find the time. Or a secluded enough spot to hide their furtive, illicit sex.

And Cory knew that it was inevitable that he was destined to be horrifically burned when it all inevitably spiraled catastrophically out of control. But he could not stop himself from stroking the toxic recipe of their needy rendezvous. Some people like to poke bears to catch a thrill. Cory found honeypots a far more enjoyable target, especially the ones with underlying daddy issues, with their accompanying unquenchable desire to be constantly stuffed to help camouflage their ugly damage.

He was rigidly helpless when Angelica looked at him with those piercing blue eyes and told him that she loved him, right before she took Cory's hardness into her mouth and expertly sucked the integrity right out of him.

II

The Scene

The actual stink of suburbia in Indiana shifts with the changing of the seasons. But generally, the odor revolves around some underlying form of combustion.

In the spring and summer, after the burden of shoveling another midwestern winter's weight out of the way, there are the enticing aromas of fire pits and barbeques sparking themselves back into life. The sweeter smells of searing flesh generally punctuate the earlier evening hours, leaving the deeper parts of the night to the glow of hardwoods smoldering cleaner than the sputtering grease.

When the humid Indiana air is enticed to move, it often catches underlying hints of chlorine lifting from the backyard pools. Or the piercing streak of freshly mown grass. And in the evenings, the breeze often helps spread the more citrusy twinge of aerosol sprays deployed to ward off the invading hordes of buzzy-fuckers hovering around, just looking for a bite.

Autumns in Indiana are a little more pungent. The smoke from the cleaner burning harder woods universally becomes cluttered with the more earthy stains of illegally burned leaves. Even within the city limits of Martinsburg, old habits die hard and that end of year Hoosier compulsion for a combustible end of summer still runs deep.

Winter starts out clean and sharp. But soon that purity is tainted by the stink of cheaply manufactured cinnamon, holiday alcohol, and sticky, bleeding evergreens.

Or the steamy, saccharine enticements of culinary memories baking in some overworked mother's kitchen.

There is some stability to be found in the seasonal symphony of that aromatic Midwestern ballet. And Cory found even more in the predictable rhythm of those summer party days filled with swimming pools. The Beverly Hills movie stars withheld their entrance on the scene until the scheduled relaxations of a pirated movie night projected itself onto a makeshift screen. But he enjoyed those, too.

It seldom mattered the hour. Or even the current state of the weather. There was almost always someone awake with whom Cory could smoke something. Or drink something. Or laugh with. The neighborhood seldom fully slept, always ebbing and flowing in the current of the newest Martinsburg drama.

Cory learned to cement those connections with casual drinking and his often-misunderstood intentions. He transitioned brilliantly into his role comprising equal parts neighborhood watch and court jester. Always looking to be productive during the daylight hours, before switching over to more offensive behaviors, to delight and entertain those living on West End Drive.

And it was all just deflection; it was all just one big 3-bedroom sized lie. Because nothing about Cory's life had ever felt genuine to him. And that uncertainty panicked him into making outlandish choices as he tried to plug the many counterfeit gaps in his disingenuous veil of happiness.

Cory could feel it all starting to slip away; he just wasn't certain if he really cared.

Cory was initially dispirited when the realization struck that he had been snared in the trap of sharing a life with someone who did not really like him. But then, Cory didn't particularly like himself, either. So on some levels he could understand the disconnect. Most days he struggled with the staleness of his circumstance considering neither one of them had started out as an honest representation. And that wasn't really any one person's fault- they had simply married embarrassingly young, back before they even had the time to figure anything out.

A house was purchased. Careers were chosen. For her, anyway. Cory bounced around a lot because he could never quite find a place in which he ever fit. It did not help his resume that he seemingly had a knack for always choosing places of employment destined to go out of business shortly after welcoming him on as part of their team.

There was a decent roof over Cory's head. There was, at that time, organically free-range food filling his belly and a shelf full of respectable booze numbing his hurt. A furry parade of interlopers tried filling the affection void. On the surface, things were comfortable by most objectively measurable benchmarks. But the simple fact was, Cory was not happy.

He felt empty and he felt insignificant. It left Cory with a lonely heart, starving for the conjoined beat of another's genuine interest. It left his intimate desires exposed and raw, hanging low and overly ripe for even a hint of attentive molestations.

And when Angelica cleverly deciphered that biological instability simmering within the hutted walls of projected suburban tranquility, she couldn't wait to exploit his weak spot growing hard. She never could resist the good fingering of a dyke, especially when she had been drinking. Even if it did technically belong to a dude.

III

The Spark

Cory first caught feelings for Angelica over a struggling autumn driveway fire shared after a long and heated Indiana summer's worth of flirting. The attraction they felt was as mutual as it was distorted. Each of them fought the initial urges to make it something more than just a conveniently casual friendship, though with each visit the conversations became more intimate. The hands came a little closer to brushing against legs hidden modestly under a garage table. Knowing glances were shared in the early morning hours as another new dawn prepared to spread its crack over a still sleeping Martinsburg.

The rhythms of their days were spent inside the confines of their unique circumstances of adulting obligations. Angelica's schedule was admittedly far more pressing than Cory's, who often spent the afternoon hours day drinking in his backyard. Or pursuing more hilariously flammable juvenile pursuits with another childish neighbor unable to work.

Angelica had children to raise half the time. And over-hyped, over-priced vacuums to sell to the more fragile and unprotected populations of Martinsburg, exchanging her charms and flirtatious vibes for a quick grab at their not always disposable incomes. There were all the old boyfriends to entertain and all the upcoming parties to plan out, responsibly scheduling the debauchery of her addictions around the ticking tocks of the work week clock.

Initially, Cory tried giving Angelica an emotional out from the hormonal morass her selfishness had created. He would always remember that conversation, sitting around the ringed fire, watching it die, honestly explaining to Angelica all the reasons he felt that she was unprepared to begin an actual adult level relationship.   But he quickly found it nearly impossible to find any reasonable traction amongst the last of the night's alcohol inhibiting her judgements.   That same clear liquid of clouded morals simultaneously pushing her to seductively spread her legs.

She continued to supplicate; he eventually surrendered.

And it wasn't long before Cory became addicted to the physical sensations of her. Theirs was an animalistic attraction based on pheromones and the desperate need to avoid the boring predictability of their comfortably parasitic Martinsburg existence.

After the heated newness of those initial penetrations cooled, relations with Angelica quickly settled into the sexual equivalent of visiting a McDonald's drive thru on a long road trip- convenient, affordable, and Cory always knew exactly what he was getting himself into. But when finally slipped the goods through regimented windows of time, he ended up somehow disappointed at the bag's appearance. It forced him to acknowledge just how badly the order had gotten fucked up. And, afterward, when indulging in a post mealtime cigarette, Cory always felt somehow unwell for having eaten out somewhere so cheap. But, a few hours later, he inexplicably found himself craving another unhealthy serving and began hitting up her phone.

It quickly became his most durable addiction.

But the underlying flatness of Angelica's personality was barely palatable to Cory, though he often pretended otherwise.   Even the synchronicity of their music failed to mesh and that annoyed him considerably.   She preferred sticking with old familiar standby's, anchoring her to earlier times, and most likely the memories of other people; he liked to explore new paths and to experience new music, always pushing to find the next great song.

The constantly conflicting music was indicative of their individual personalities. Angelica was always quick to settle, while Cory remained determined to always find something better.   Mediocre was enough to sustain her; his fires needed substantially more fuel.

Maybe it was the interference of her voracious appetite for intoxicating substances that most influenced that disparity. Not that Cory was some outlandishly puritanical example- he could drink with the best of them and was often the last man literally standing. He just didn't need all the accompanying powders or the pills like she seemingly did, in order to simply function.

Overall, there were only little snippets of time where Cory truly liked being with her. It was somewhere between not necessarily sober, but not yet blackout drunk.   And those windows only grew smaller the more time they spent together, making the maintenance of even a friendship an impossibly challenging endeavor.

He just didn't really care. Because in the crushing boredom of Martinsburg suburbia, being manipulated was somehow more enticing than being ignored.

IV

The Grind

"You realize that you're raising two shitty kids, right?"

In that heated moment, Cory had committed the cardinal sin when fucking someone else's baby mama- under no circumstances do you ever criticize the kids. Even when their lies and little manipulative games are so blatantly apparent it's laughable. Even when the effects of those bad behaviors leak out and they are caught red handed, again, spying on naked relations.

And that baffling disparity between truth and insulation was incredibly frustrating for Cory as he constantly tried balancing the equation of a clear reality with Angelica's skewed and twisted manipulations of perception.

In fact, it drove him fucking nuts.

"Shut the fuck up! You're not even their dad!" came Angelica's shortsighted biological retort.

Cory further complicated the tense atmosphere by letting the slightest bit of laughter escape his face, triggered by the sheer ridiculousness of her supposed insult.

Shortly after he laughed, a glass ashtray went flying by his head, shattering against the wall behind him. As she often did in moments of escalated turmoil, Angelica reverted to committing physical acts of retaliation against Cory's brute verbal honesty. Thankfully, she was already bordering on blacking out when she made her newest pitch, so her aim was off just enough that Cory avoided serious injury.

Unlike the time she had drunkenly kicked Cory in the balls, simply because he held on to her purse strap to keep her from driving blackout drunk. There had been kicks and fists and shoves, none of which ever drew a response from Cory. He knew full well the second he lifted a finger, even if it was in self-defense, he would most certainly be spending a significant amount of time in a Martinsburg holding cell.

Within the stoic, stiff upper-lipped classes of the Martinsburg society, domestic abuse was universally seen as a one-way street. Men are universally considered to be at fault, regardless of any evidence to the contrary. And any man who foolishly allowed himself to seek help for any form of abuse was immediately seen as being some weak. Because "real men" were expected to suffer in silence.

On the night of the flying ashtray, Cory reached the limit of his patience with Angelica's near total lack of parenting skills. Because she was refusing to see objectively just how shitty things had turned, and how wildly out of control things were spinning. Or maybe on some levels she did see it, only to subversively twist and deflect it back so that the blame rested squarely on Cory.

He ultimately became sort of a bad parenting goldilocks- he was either too rigid, or too soft. Too demanding, or too flexible. Angelica's benchmark for parenting decisions shifted constantly, seemingly on a whim, and that volatile unpredictability left Cody frustrated at his inability to crack her indecipherable code of expectation.

In ways he could never reasonably explain, or even fully understand, Cory blinked and discovered that he was suddenly somehow responsible for raising two shitty kids, spawned from two shitty fathers. He was pulled into the orbit of the chaos spawned from her ridiculously flawed parenting and the shockingly predictable repercussions. Cory found himself burdened to somehow fix things before it was too late and the world was doomed to admit two more self-centered, manipulative assholes.

He also felt himself sacrificing his future for the promise of theirs. He exhausted himself constantly trying to build a clean, stable life while everyone else was trying to just get high. Or fat. Or fucked.

Cory was trapped in an unhealthy environment where telling the truth was mystifyingly considered abuse. He was constantly belittled and dismissed.   His calls of caution were religiously ignored and when the outcomes he had predicted came to fruition, he was blamed for that, too.

By the time Cory realized he was caught trying to raise three children, given how childishly Angelica behaved, he began to suspect that it was over.

He just couldn't bring himself to say it quite yet.

V

The Break

"You have 24 hours to get your essentials out. You can make arrangements for the rest."

A Christmas morning text message was Cory's only present that year, despite having funded the lion's share of the gifts stacked neatly under the tree. All those beautifully wrapped and labeled packages for people who simply did not appreciate his efforts sat destined to be opened without him. Not that he particularly cared; it was just more crap that nobody really wanted, or needed. But everyone still expected to see on the morning of some strange savior's birth.

Despite the more reasonable angels of Cory's financial sensibilities, he had caved that year and given in to the materialistic frenzy of plastic people unwrapping their plastic offerings to fill the noticeable gaps in their plastic, unfulfilled little lives. And it left him feeling empty and unsettled, priming the pump for what would prove to be the bookend argument in a relationship reaching its collapse.

They spent a last night together and awoke to an early morning disagreement. Cory, not wanting to stoke the toxic fires of her unreasonable drama, removed himself from the situation, thinking it was the only possible move to diffuse the situation. But Angelica jumped at the opportunity and sent him that cowardly text message instead of handling things like an adult. Because that would have required a maturity that Angelica quite clearly lacked.

Cory was instantly ostracized, by both family and supposed friends, as the demarcation lines of shattering allegiances were drawn. Angelica had manipulated the lion's share of their friends to her orbital influence, regaling them with fanciful tales of supposed abuses that never actually occurred.

Like how she was never "allowed" to spend any time with any of her friends, while consistently overlooking the little detail that Angelica never once even mentioned her intentions. She just assumed that Cory would say no and then got angry at him for not letting her do something he didn't even know she wanted to pursue.

Admittedly, Cory wasn't a fan of most of Angelica's friends. They were a tragically flawed parade of broken and damaged people who never expressed much interest in improving themselves. Most of that energy was instead redirected into their shady efforts of attempting to gain entrance into Angelica's pants, attention in which she found herself constantly reveling. Their drunken flirtations served to feed her deep-seated need for validation and she ravenously consumed their misguided affections.

But he never once said that she couldn't spend time with them. Even after the "girls' night out" night when she was dropped off blackout drunk, spewing vile insults at Cory, when not throwing actual objects. The accusations began flying simply because Cory had reasonably suggested maybe she should sober up a little in the backyard before saying goodnight to the kids. The same kids who had spent the entire night wondering and worrying about their mother's noticeable absence. The same kids who had to listen to her moan and piss her way through another night spent sprawled naked on the floor, a puke bucket placed by her head.

And yet somehow, all that was somehow Cory's fault, too. But then, he was always awarded the blame when Angelica spun off the rails and it frustrated Cory that she always managed to somehow dodge responsibility for her actions.

She also claimed the entirety of their nest egg, entitling herself to all the available resources, most of which she did not earn honestly. Angelica claimed that she would need it for the kids who had conveniently been added to the equation as the household split, though he knew most of it would go instead to funding the demands of her many self-medicating requirements.

Cory, having grown weary of her manipulations, did not really put up much of a fight. There wasn't much that he wanted and even less that he viewed as salvageable. She could have everything as far as he was concerned. Well, everything but his integrity. Because in the end, he knew that he had been correct in all his predictions and there was nothing that Angelica could ever say or do to change that.

The truth was the truth and while Angelica attempted her alcoholic best to block it all out, or somehow manipulate it into a more personally flattering incarnation, Cory chose to embrace it. That honesty was the chosen hill upon which he would give his last, even if it proved to be his downfall.

Instead of wallowing, or following Angelica's lead of trying to find answers inside a bottle, Cory instead prepared himself to start over, again, with no real resources. He quickly faced the realization that he would have to claw his way back up to the lower echelons of middle class all on his own.

And Cory struggled.

It was during those dark days he finally understood that one cannot count on the durability of intimate strangers when grinding out the existence of poverty. Everybody was too busy caught pursuing their own responsibilities to be bothered with throwing any sort of meaningful lifeline his way. Especially not to a person who had so egregiously sabotaged his life for the sake of dishonest enticements.

As the reality of that lesson began to sink into the festering wounds, so raw and seeping, it was already too late. Cory's fate had been sealed the very moment his lips had touched hers.

And he could only blame himself.

VI

The Fall

The clock on the living room wall was ticking out of time.

But so, too, was Cory.

His only company in that smoky room was the obscure muffle of his favorite music playing through the tobacco haze hanging low and the right hand millimetered twists of metallic surrender.

Cory looked down at his own useless hands, twitching at the table's edge. Then his unfocused gaze shifted up to the hands on the wall, lying to that clock's face.

More than half of his life had gone by, stained by the pallor of the cliché and served out daily in sacrificially-sized bites of his deeply ingrained Martinsburg culpability. It was within that binding palette of expectation that Cory finally recognized the true color of his failure. It was the same sickly tint that had consistently encroached over every outlined figure foolish enough to have ever loved him.

Cory had sold his potential embarrassingly cheap for the uninhibited promise of new sensations tickling naked flesh blushing warm. He had sacrificed his then far off "golden years" for a temporarily closer embrace. And then he mistakenly blinked. Because just that quickly, those very same years came tapping at his front door, demanding explanation for being abandoned to starve.

It had all started with a simple, infectious kiss that was the genesis of his fallibility. That intimate moment where he stepped off the unstable ledge of his impure privilege and right into the free fall embrace of eternal sabotage.

In the end, she was not responsible for his destruction; he had chosen instead to demolish himself. He jumped brazenly into the oblivion of his inconsequentiality rather than to stay behind, just to feel it all burn down around him. He feared the emptiness of the fall far less than he did the stinging bite of the flames.

It was much easier to just let go.

And so, he did.

But the music continued to play. Right up until when it didn't. The haze cleared. Cluttered rooms were cleaned. Walls, repainted. A simple life scrubbed away in fresh coats of uncomfortable disclosures.

And Martinsburg, Indiana neither wept, nor acknowledged. It continued as it always had, under the guiding influence of its deeply refined Hoosier stoicism; it simply did not understand how to be anything different.

People returned to work. Relationships evolved. Bridges were burnt and hastily rebuilt. Injustices ran rampant through countless petty dramas playing out daily in thousands of little houses to the endless amusement of their fishbowled inhabitants.

Unstoppable. Unforgiving. Unremarkable.

But that is just life in another flyover town.

Or at least, so they say…

TypewriterFox.com